Hamilton's Heber Flashes

Hamilton's Heber Flashes

R Kuppuswamy

ISBN:	Hardcover	978-1-4828-8426-5
	Softcover	978-1-4828-8425-8
	eBook	978-1-4828-8424-1

Print information available on the last page.

To order additional copies of this book, contact
Partridge India
000 800 10062 62
orders.india@partridgepublishing.com

www.partridgepublishing.com/india

Contents

Part One

Part Three

Part Four

This book, not designed to

conform to any particular

literary genre,

is dedicated

to

Prof Bennet Albert

of

Madras Christian College

and

my classmates.

1968

This is brought out in love for my

Dad, David Rajappa Pillai

and

Mom, Esther Rani Taima

Thanked for assistance

my

Wife, Jayasheeli

Son, Raja Prabhu

and

the great computer.

Hamilton

Hamilton is a student of Madras Christian College, Tambaram. He studied there when Dr Chandran Devanesan was the principal; Dr Macphail, the professor; and Dr Mithra Agustin, the warden. In this college, the hostels are called 'halls'. Bishop Heber Hall is one of the three; the other two, St Thomas Hall and Selaiyur Hall. Lately, St Martin Hall was added. And that is for women.

Each hall is separate situated over a 200 metres apart. From the halls, the college main block is at five minutes on foot.

Mastered in 1968, Hamilton started off with teaching. Teaching English at an arts college in Coimbatore was no doubt sweet, but he chose not to take it up for his life's career. Soon, he wrote a competitive exam, came out successful, and got placed as a government executive.

His executive days were funny; the most enjoyable was the fun of being shifted from one district to another. These districts did him nothing new, just raised his age; some districts up by one year, and some by one more. After the district years, he landed up at Madras, the state's capital city.

At Madras, things were funnier. He sat on and rose from seat to seat in a series of in-city transfers to offices, lying on either side of the Mount Road from Saidapet to the Marina Beach. Here, the seat spans in most posts were brief. The briefest: sixty days.

Finally, he was drawn into the chief power centre—the St George Fort.

The fort days were the funniest. The files swallowed the first half, and the meetings swallowed the second half of the work time. With the days that passed at the fort in Hamilton, there had occurred a number of transformations. The apparent were his hair had gone grey, and skin shrunk into furrows.

We know in the world, all things age. But there is one thing that doesn't. What is that? That is the government. It is young, always young—and cute too. It is particularly cute in remembering the seat-leaving dates of its work force.

When Hamilton's age struck sixty, and when he heard that sound, it was an evening. It was that evening of that day he was overjoyed that after a gap of thirty-eight years, his right to himself had become his own again.

Rid of office, life became different. It had to be lived differently most of the time, either bound up at home or loosened out into the city. Both were fine in the first few days, then a bore. We know what the present Madras is, and what in future it is going to be for road and traffic, crowd and noise and heat and dust.

Unable to love the city like he used to in his young days, Hamilton desired a change of place. What he desired at heart grew into a decision. For him, it is a great decision because it is that decision that carried him eight thousand five hundred feet up above the sea level. Now, in Ooty, that is cool and at his cottage, which is green, Hamilton is sipping tea.

Do you know what stirs deep inside a government man? A longing—a longing to be free and happy. For him, to be free predominantly means not having to work under a boss who knows, in tension, only to bark. To be happy means using all that he has as he likes.

In the case of Hamilton, what does he have? Nothing. Nothing much compared to others. Yet he has one thing. What? Time. The time after superannuation. With all his pockets so full with free time, what does Hamilton do? He spends. How? Mostly watching like a child the Ooty profusion of flowers in their ravishing hues and dazzling designs, gazing at the clouds sporting in the sky, riding the heritage train that dances merrily through the tunnels. In the rose garden, walking with friends among the multi-coloured blooms, battling with the blinding mist in an uphill trek to the crest; and back at the cottage, fresh after a bath, playing on the keyboard the songs of his teens.

Of all things man enjoys, what does he enjoy the most? It is fun, which fortunately is nobody's monopoly. It lies spread all the world over. To seek the best, Hamilton tours.

As a man of rest at his magnificent valley—the second largest in the world—and as one who travels to places worth a visit, whenever prompted, Hamilton writes. Here on the pages that follow, he comes out with a bit of the past he could recall, and a little of the future he could imagine.

Part One

Chapter 1

The Hall and Fun

A couple of centuries ago, there was, at Oxford, a young man. A doctorate in divinity, he came to Calcutta as its bishop. His diocese was vast comprising India, Ceylon, and Australia. As a missionary, he found the people of Madras good, and preached them the gospel of Christ and his salvation.

That bishop is Bishop Gerald Heber, after whom Hamilton's hall has been named. Of all the male halls, Heber is known for its great funs, but those funs are not open to all. To get them to enjoy, there are conditions to be fulfilled; of course, not many, only two. One is you should know how to laugh, another, you should know how to think. Since thinking is not generally one of what people like, that is not taken up for a serious assessment. You are checked mainly for your laugh status. In that, however, you shouldn't test negative.

As a preliminary to the new academic year in the hall, a series of funs are played on the new boys. These fun makers are inventive as also educative. Their inventiveness never goes erratic. It is carefully guarded by the code of Heber decorum.

Some ask, 'In what way is fun useful?' Hamilton answers, 'In many ways.' Fun is not teasing, not bullying; It is an exchange of joy. When that joy passes into the youngsters, it warms them up. The joy warmed young man at study lights upon a role model. That role model is his mold into which he pours himself. There in that mold, he takes his shape.

College is for work, and hall for rest, think some. Wrong. In the process of learning, college and hall play each a part. While college stuffs the head, it is hall that digests it. If the hall part of life is not lived squarely, the yield of the college part will be, but poor.

Chapter 2

The Hat Night

In Heber Hall, the concluding fun day is special. That day, in the evening, the fun sources are activated, mainly the fish pond. It is filled with water mixed with a spoon of powder colour. In that, the freshers are given a ducking. When dragged out, unable to bear their own look, they rush up for an emergency bath. In a few minutes, they come back marching down in groups like the heavenly saints in white. Paper hats on heads, an important ceremonial feature to mark the climax of the season's fun, they gather in the hall yard.

Then they climb the stage on which the eyes of the seniors and those of the juniors intermingle. Swayed by emotion, the seniors hug the juniors. When the juniors returned the hug, the scene went wild. Overwhelmed with the hugs, those on the stage melted into tears. While at the tears' peak, they felt something binding. It took them not long to realise what it was that bound. It was the love of Heber. It bound their hearts with so much love that they might not forget these sweet moments due to the passage of what we call time.

The youngsters, still in the warmth of the hug, moved on to the lawn where, under the colourful illumination, was the dinner. Another such dinner so grand, Hamilton never enjoyed before or would enjoy again.

The fun of the night that passed with the hats on heads—hat night is how it is called—is a turning point. The tears on the stage and the dinner on the lawn meant something truly great.

Chapter 3

Freedom and Joy

The next morning, Heber had become a hall of new love, new friendship, new freedom, and a hall devoted wholeheartedly to the pursuit of its cherished goals.

In the campus were buildings. Some huge like the main block, the science blocks, and the arts blocks. The rest, like the staff quarters, were small. But what were they all doing? They were doing their assigned job of simply being where they had been built, whereas Heber had a purpose relating to each of its boys and promoted their interests with zeal.

Hamilton, who was Heber's pet, had a wide range of interests—interests in composing songs, practising music, researching on Nostradamus, and experimenting on the truths about the curious powers of the things in the shapes of pyramid. Since he needed his room for the play of all his interests, it was not a mere cell of books, it was much more—even an art museum and a creative workshop.

The buildings and the structures, no matter how big, including the principal's bungalow, seemed to Hamilton as satellites orbiting his mansion on their ordained circles. The postgraduate house was the hub. Two double three its heart. And Hamilton was at its centre ruling the whole hall as its prince.

It was at this habitation that he spent the last two of his unforgettable student years. In the portico, memorizing poetry; on the compound wall, doing homework; upon the trees, doing circus; and along the corridor, playing guitar—all these until sundown, then Hamilton throws off his guitar to the farthest of his back.

After dinner when the study time nears, he, like the other boys, withdraws into the room, leaving it ajar for the deputy warden on rounds to take a quick look and go his way quietly. The deputy warden gone, the doors are shut. Hours pass, night succumbs to stillness; and in his room, on Hamilton's mind, opens a new world—a new universe rather. In that universe, in a poetic flight with Shelley, he is filled with the thrill of soaring higher and higher.

We know where there are colleges, by their side stand hostels. In the city of Madras are hostels in hundreds, but all rocked by traffic, noise, and human bustle. Hamilton's hall is an exception. Nowhere else is the hall seclusion so undisturbed, and the room privacy so unviolated. For a student to stay in and to study, Hamilton would say, Heber, by all standards, is the finest.

Chapter 4

The Mornings

This college is a forest. You may call it also a park. In winter, so lush. Before it is light, if you get up and go out, you can see how balmy is the morning that turns slowly into brightness, and how cool is the wind that blows gently through the verdant leaves. You can see in the pale glimmer of dawn the beauty of the lawns strewn with pearls and pearls of dews. The whole forest is serene. Only the calls of birds, one bird calling here and another, there, waking up the youths still buoyant on their sleep.

Walk to that familiar tree, which is behind the tennis court. Sit under, let the flowers, on your face, breathe their fragrance with a soft touch. Look up, look around, look up again. You see that there, over there, there on the tree, the same little bird, which often comes flying down to the windowsill of Hamilton's room. What is it doing there now? It is sending the day's first admiration to its sweetheart on another tree between St Thomas Hall and Selaiyur Hall.

Hamilton's hallmates were brilliant, all of them. They were full with the highest of the future plans. At sunrise, we can watch them, some on a run in the playground pouring countless drums of sweat, some doing pull-ups with a couple of eggs inside, some on the cement bench masticating a book word by word, some on the top of a tall tree downloading into their heads the contents of the Competition Master.

The tenacity in the case of some boys made an ever-talked college talk. One boy in Hamilton's batch absconded. It was whispered he had run away with a girl. After some days, the boy returned and invited his friends for a tea. When his friends went to see that girl he had brainwashed in such a short time, the poor boy, to the tea, came alone with a new story. To the frustration and surprise of the gathering, he narrated that the tea was not for what his friends had thought. It was for his selection for an All India Service, and for his going to become the auditor general of West Bengal.

Chapter 5

Visit England

Of all the academic subjects, the most fascinating is literature. The proper way to study it is to study it into its depth. To study into its depth, we should study it in the true setting of its conception. But it is not done. Not just possible. And so, literature in the true sense, is neither studied nor understood.

In our system, it is a printed matter read aloud, listened to, essays prepared, answers written; and at last the student, if lucky, passed, if not, failed. That is the meaning of literature in our exam-oriented university sense. The desire of Hamilton is that it should mean more.

Literature buds from the root of the author in a mood of a creative wizardry. The root of the author is in his native background. To gain the right knowledge of that background, we should visit the place of his birth and upbringing. Then why the students of English Literature shouldn't pay a visit to England?

What a joy it will be to fly in a group from Delhi to London in the British Airways! After lunch at the Buckingham Palace with Her Highness, the Queen of England, what a thrill it will be to visit the places where Shakespeare and Anne Boleyn met, where Johnson and Boswell chatted, where Lamb and Mary wrote *The Tales*, where T.S. Eliot toured his *Waste Land*, and where Doris May Lessing brought out her *Golden Notebook!*

After a hectic twenty-one days of exploring England, what a fine thing it will feel to return, not by the same airways but by another. Not straight back to Delhi, but via Bombay. And what a fulfillment it will be to stay a couple of days there. Not in a star hotel where guns may shoot, bombs may burst, and rivers of blood may flow. At Raj Bhavan on Malabar Hill, jutting out in a scenic view all safe into the Arabian Sea. In the morning, after breakfast with His Excellency, the Governor of Maharashtra, visit the Gateway of India, Elephanta Caves, Prince of Wales Museum, and go a good shopping at Bhagat Singh Marg. Chor Bazaar, Phonix Market, And Oberoi Mall.

Next day, return. With the three weeks and two days of trans-continental sensation craving to find a vent, when you are back in the class tired and fresh, how do you think that day would pass? No lesson. Absolutely no. Only chat and laugh, except of course in the most feared class of Prof Bennet Albert.

Chapter 6

The Campus Rumours

The campus was lively. Mostly the rumours made it so. Of the rumours, one was to the department of botany, in the night hours, spirit boars come. Some of the boars are black like soot, and some white like snow. They assemble in the lab. Then from the lab, stalk onto the road; and there, in pairs, they waltz. At that time, if you go there alone, they welcome you with joy and hug you with a grin.

This rumour made its hurried rounds among the tender ears of the boys and girls.

The botany lab area was a bit extra dim, no doubt. That was for the surrounding dense-leafed giant trees. About having seen the boars, there was never an eyewitness. More often than others, Hamilton rambles that side to cool down his head gone hot with reading the poets like Lord Byron. But not once was he accosted by a boar of any colour—black like soot or white like snow.

Chapter 7

In the Dining Hall

Watching the moon that shines from the cloudless sky above and hearing the boughs that rustle around, Hamilton plods along the byway at a slow pace to the mess. In the mess that is busy, none takes notice of him. For the timely diners, the bond of friendship with the late coming hallmates always suffers a cut.

Our eating style is inimitable. The fingers are our fork and knife, spoon and chopstick, tong and shear. Sometimes, we dip the forearm the whole length into the plate. So the pre and post meal handwash is a table must. Not washing, objectionably unIndian.

His forefingers wet, Hamilton barges in and finds a seat. Elbows on the table, his eyes have swept not half across the dining hall when Captain, the tallest of the mess staff, is already there with a dish in hand for Hamilton to deal with.

In the mess, it is not always the students who dine. Their masters also join, the bachelor masters regularly, and the married masters when alone. If the teachers and students could do the same work in the same place at the same time together without any predicament, you can see them do that so well in the mess.

Dining is a self-directed piece of execution. In that, without exception, all the hall boys are proficient. They know the chicken full book, chapter by chapter and page by page. They can annotate in the chicken any sentence anywhere unerringly.

The prospective builders of India, Sri Lanka, Malaysia, Indonesia, Philippines, Singapore, China, Mongolia, Hong Kong, and other countries are there in the dining rows.

Watch their sitting, starting, and handling of the mess stuff. It is a multitude of races converged on food and occupied on various styles of biting, chewing, and relishing. When they finish, they finish with a touch of clinical accuracy.

The yellow boys, all of them, are avowed consumers of beasts and birds. They however don't spare flora. From the damp recesses of the campus jungle, they brought to the mess certain green leaves, which they munched side by side. When asked, it was explained. They are not just leaves, they are the energy-giving herbals essential to fight their judo and wushu.

Then after dinner, on the way back to their rooms, comes the crowning pitch. What is that? That belch, that tremor-like eruption proclaiming that the important job of the evening is over.

It was pleasant talking to the yellow youngsters. If we talk, they would talk back not instantly. To start a talk, their vocal system would take time. Once started, the talk won't end shortly. It would jump straight on the Chinese famous dishes like spring rolls, chow mein, ma po tofu, sweet and sour pork, Peking roasted duck, and run the whole day without stopping.

Their phonetic style was excellent. It was true to Daniel Jones word for word. And their food style was fast. It was true to Genghis Khan bone for bone.

Chapter 8

Genghis Khan

We know who Genghis Khan is. He is a king of China. This name, Genghis Khan, was not an ordinary name. It was equal to thunder that sent shock waves into spine. But that was when Khan was alive. Not now.

What is funny about the kings is that the great kings, they too, die. Because they are kings, their death is not the same as the death of others. For the kings, it is not actually a death, it is a transit. Transit from their ancestral palace to the library. In the library, they take the seat the librarian allots. On that seat, they don't keep quiet. Far from it, they rule—rule like while alive. Most kings capture places. They have captured the educational institutions and the book stalls. The Higginbothams are their fort away from fort.

The kings were dreamers, and so were also the men of non-kingly greatness. They dreamt that they should be feared and venerated even after their death. So the dead great men are dominant. Intrusive, some even an annoyance. The youngsters have to take them to the central part of their brain, keep chained to their memory, escort safely to the examination and interview halls, and there produce when called out to.

There are some great men who don't die a complete death. Because the death they die is an incomplete death, they get up. They get up every time they are remembered by the people, positively for their birthdays. When they get up, it is a great occasion. Carousals are held, crackers are fired, and in the sky launched an endless number of country rockets that burst into domes of spectacular galaxy.

Chapter 9

The Diamond Youths

The rulers who ruled found it a pleasure to rule this country because it is vast and beautiful. The border north is mount-locked and snow-capped. The peninsular south is sea-hedged and wave-splashed. The inland is rich with everything that a man would like and a woman would desire.

All countries loved India. They loved for different purposes. Some to visit, some to play with, some to flirt with, some to enjoy a company, some to have, and some to own. Only a few to get away contented with a bare look.

Africa also loved, but its love was not carnal, not shaded by anything unseemly. It was pure and platonic. Africa is one of the best continents in the world. Its people are harmless. They never overran India, laid a city waste, stormed a fortress, or razed a shrine to the ground.

Some young men from the diamond continent also were at Heber. These were the real men. For them, nothing is too heavy to lift or too strong to break. Always happy and high-spirited, not merely consummate practitioners of life's youthful arts.

Also, they are the believers of practical values, a good education, a good job, and a good earning. If it is a friendship, it's a good friendship. If a fight, a good fight. If a peace, it's a good piece. If fun, it's a good fun. They didn't want life to mean anything more.

Their philosophy is, 'In life, there is nothing to understand, but there is so much to live. No man ever lived happily having first understood life. If you think about life, it is a bewilderment. If you live, it is a pleasure. If you think too much, it is a hell. If you just live, it is paradise.'

No believers in dreams or in vain talks, they limit to looking at things just as what they mean to a normal human being at the first natural glance.

The diamond young men were no way a disturbance to any. They loved the Indian boys and invited them home to their country. Hamilton was invited more than once. But then, he couldn't say Yes or No. When invited fondly for Christmas, he thought a minute and asked himself, 'Accepting the invitation, if I go with them, what shall I see there?'

It was a continent of multi-national colonies like India was. There should be cities with old buildings, sandstone structures, red brick courts, high-walled jails, uncared roads, abandoned lanes. There should be politicians and businessmen luxuriating on the sweat of the poor, the same way as is going on in India.

In India, the foreigners lifted cattle, women, and land. In Africa, they wouldn't have done anything different. There, also, they would have lifted these usual three: cattle, women, and land. And one more additionally, diamond. There, like here, the foreigners would have used the native people as buyers of their textiles, and as killers to kill themselves. No chance for anything else to have existed or happened.

Africa is a continent of the least spoiled natural beauty. One should see that, they say. Deep at heart, Hamilton had a wish to visit. But its realisation was, for some reason or other, getting put on hold. The time has finally come. Now he can go happily. To help him, there is a boy, a Heber boy, as the deputy prime minister of Uganda. A gentle kind, not the kind of man Idi Amin was.

Chapter 10

Africa and Maths

Heber food was intercontinental, yet, not in the fullest sense. It failed to please the diamond youngsters. It was but not an issue for them. They knew cooking and could easily cook their native food here. But rules said 'not in the hall'. Then some of them quit Heber for private accommodations.

There, they ate well, played well, studied well, watched things closely, and pitied the Indian boys for reading so long and so hard daily.

Their English was stylish, though grammar-free. Exempt from the dictates of grammar, the diamond young men use that language as a tool, just a tool. They don't worship English.

We hear that mathematics is the queen of sciences, but the diamond owners hate that queen. Said an Algerian lad, 'If you have interest, do maths for research. If it is not difficult, do to join maths related jobs in banks. But doing it for academic necessity is bad.' He went on to add, 'Still if done, it will cause a serious damage to the brain.' The simple heads have understood that, but not the fathomless ones. Had Einstein understood that instead of taxing his thinking skills beyond all the human limits, he would have readily accepted the offer of the presidentship of Israel, and visited all countries at the government's cost.

One diamond student found Pythagoras tough. From the height of his wrath, he declared, 'Maths is a devilry of a wrong-headed nut. It is foolish to do maths.'

Some people think that the entire life is in algebra, calculus, trigonometry, or netwok geometry. The diamond young men warn us, 'Be advised, it is not in these things.' Then where? 'It is in a good sleep, in a good run, in a good wrestle, or in a good swim. When feeling cold, life is in a hot tea. When feeling hot, it is in a cold ice cream. When feeling neither hot nor cold, we should understand, it is in a cup of fresh apple juice.'

'What we like, we should do; and what we don't, we shouldn't.' It is their way.

But most of the people in the world don't think so. They think that all that they think are of little avail unless approved by a third party. In their own thinking, they have no belief. Their belief is that they have the right only to be wrong, and that their right to rightness is with somebody else always.

Chapter 11

The Food and its Power

Nature produced food that the early man ate and lived. When the later man produced it himself, it ceased to be good. No food value, no food content, no food taste, only the nauseating smell of agro-fertilizers. Incredible, but is said in the food we eat, there is poison. It is mixed at two stages: one, at the base stage; another, at the preparation stage. The base stage poison is in the fertilizer treated soil, and the preparation stage poison is in the chemical mixed oil.

Yet, on this score, we need not panic or blame the food makers. The food makers are good people. They love us. They want us. They want us to live, live in good health until 3000 AD. That is why, to protect our life, on the consumer goods they display the Date of Expiry.

The real food, the natural one, has left us long ago. When it left, it left with the arrival of a science called agricultural science. What is agricultural science? To tell the truth, it is the science of poison that kills the people slowly after killing the pests quickly. Though the food is poisonous, to dispose it, we have not discovered a new way. The only way known to us is just to eat it. Refusing to eat it is refusing to live the days it allows.

Chapter 12

Man and Religion

The diamond youngsters were known not only for the strength of physique, but the fear of God as well. They were spiritual keenly interested in gospel truths. Not like the non-diamond guys whom, on Sundays, we can't see in churches.

Church comes under the subject of religion. What is religion? It is something God only knows. Some people say that they also know. To know if they know, we should hear them. Only hear, not speak. If you speak back and raise doubts, it means you are whipping up a headache. So the knowledge of religion lies jammed somewhere between what should not be questioned and what could not be answered.

Some say religion thrives within a protected light, some say protected darkness, some say protected loudness, some say protected dumbness, some say protected cunning, and some say protected cheating. Which is correct? All of them, or some of them or none of them? No one knows for certain.

But one thing is clear—crystal clear. Religion is not a unifier, it is a divider. Not a life giver, it is a man killer, a great divider, a great killer. It has been that ever since it came into being.

Religion is a world of laws, clever laws. It grants limitless right to obey. To know no right, to speak no right, to question no right. Our limit, as regards religion, ends with playing yes man for every word of the religious head. We are more than happy and more than contented to have the privilege to say a ready yes since it is feared what lies outside that yes is the highway to hell. What is hell? Has anyone seen it? Why seeing and all? Not necessary. To believe needs no seeing, no verifying. Without seeing and without verifying once, we know what it is. What is it? It is a place where, for the purpose of burning, bad men are used as coal. Who is a bad man? Of a bad man, every religion has a definition of its own. To burn the bad men from all religions, Hamilton guesses, for each religion, there should be a separate burner in hell.

There are many religions in the world. Each one has an independent route, which is sensitive. The routes should not cross or run close. In case they do, there is a clash.

Religion is used for diverse purposes including for naming schools, colleges, and universities in which all sorts of things are taught, but not religion. Why not taught? If taught as a subject, and if the students are turned out with certificates, diplomas, graduations, post-graduations, and even doctorates, they will get no job. Not in the government, not in the private. The knowledge of God gets you no job. If you want to be selected as a government man, you can be qualified in any subject except in what speaks of your eternal welfare.

Religion is a bridle that controls the world. Man fears religion. He fears so much that he doesn't start anything without its green signal. It is so powerful. If it is powerless, it is powerless rarely like where a boy and a girl fall in love or a man and a woman elope.

Religion is not something conceded on demand or presented as a gift. It runs with time, travels with society, lives with family, and jumps into man the day he is named. With that naming, he becomes his religion, which sticks on to him till he is dead and forgotten.

Everyone carries a religion in his name. Outside religion, no man is possible, no woman is possible, also no name is possible.

Religion is a bridge. Without it, we can have no link with the country, with the society, with the individuals, and with ourselves. We are seen through our religion. Understood too.

We can say and agree that all religions are the same speaking about love. Though they speak about love—only love—we can't belong to all. We can belong to only one, one at a time. That is the law—universal law on religion.

A person can be more than one in many things. Even in country. Not in religion. No one can be bi-religious or tri-religious. It is a single track until altered.

Religion is there rather for belonging than following. Belonging is the utmost we do to religion. If the style of our belonging is questioned, our belonging gets emotionally hot, sometimes at the expense of our right to belong.

In the matter of religion, you can't be silent. You can't say you don't want a religion and don't want to belong to any. Whether you like it or not, you should take one, and belong to one. If you refuse to take and refuse to belong, religion will not wait for your consent. It has ways, ineludible ways, to make you take and make you belong.

Chapter 13

The Ghosts

Belief substitutes what can't be proved by science. One of our beliefs is ghosts exist. They exist in all countries and love people—love particularly those people who are new.

For meeting the new people, the Indian ghosts started to move westward half century ago. The Chinese ghosts have just begun to cross their border.

The western writers and filmmakers have a great liking and high regard for ghosts. They treat them as their fellow humans, and in their fictions and movies, assign them the roles of heroes and heroines. They want to use them for other purposes too. To learn more about how far the ghosts would suit the other purposes, these writers and filmmakers visit places far and wide.

The best place for ghost information inside India is Dumas Beach in Gujarat. Outside India, Bermuda, but to these two places, they don't go. They fear. They fear that in Dumas Beach, they would be sucked into the seawaters, and in Bermuda, swallowed up in the whirlpools.

The ghosts love to be always joyful. For them to be so, to say the least, the countries should be old and their capitals dungeon-like. The palaces there should abound in myths of kings no longer alive visiting at nights; the buried emperors in golden headdress riding fiery chariot pulled by dark horses; apparition of decapitated preacher carrying its head around followed by a large dog; in ancient forts, sound of footsteps coming from nowhere; woman killed and thrown into well, rising at night and counting to nine before shrieking and returning to the bottom; voices heard in the air about concealed murders and covered up burials; graveyards opening and the spirits of dead men coming out and fighting. For the ghosts to be more joyful, the people there should be prone to delirious daydreams and convulsive night fits.

The countries, which are young and neat, bright and smart, fast and sharp, the ghosts won't like.

We think that the young countries should have made their progress only economically, and in the ghost field lag behind. Not correct. In spirit knowledge too, they have grown potent. They compete with the old countries over the techniques of black arts like witchcrafts and sorcery. And with them, the horror activities are growing spiritually as fast as commercially.

Ours, down the recent decades, has been an all round growth, knowledge explosion echoing everywhere. Get into the cabin of a quiet browsing centre, spend a couple of hours there. Yahoo will tell you, in ghost knowledge, how much advanced we are—the people of the twenty first century.

Chapter 14

Education

Education is our second breath, likely to become the first soon, that the people know. In the current world, all people. They also know that it is growing. Growing, but mostly at the hands of Shylocks.

'Owning an educational institution', goes a talk, 'is owning a private security press.'

For their children's education, the parents are prepared to spend any sum of money. A young boy or a young girl, therefore, is like a goose that lays golden currency. To scoop that currency, in every main road town has come up a college; in every branch road village, a high school; in every street, an elementary school; and in every lane, a nursery.

We all know the Indian parents are the second highest in child production. Still, for children, there is a shortage. The educationists want more and more of boys and girls. But parents couldn't supply. To wrest them from the available stock, the schools, colleges, and universities give publicity like it is given to boost the sale of T-shirt and jeans pant, leather shoes, and nylon socks, toothpaste, and detergent powder, nail polish, and ladies' handbag.

Educational growth is a mad growth. At present, one month is enough to put up a shed, recruit teachers, canvass students, and complete admissions. Without office rooms, staff rooms, classrooms, libraries, laboratories, canteens, toilets, and also without government license, schools, colleges, and universities can run.

In such wonder institutions, the youngsters study and pass. Some with distinctions. But people ask, 'What is the use of these distinctions?' Are these distinction holders the top people in our nation, in our state, in our district, in our taluk, in our firka, in our village, or at least in our municipal ward?

We are in the days of bachelors and masters of arts, sciences, and businesses added to masters and doctors of philosophy, and letters produced in the universities of India as fast and as much as China produces fire crackers, fire sparklers, fire flowers, fire fountains, fire rockets, fire dynamites, and fire mines in its cottage industry.

People think education is a departure from dark to light, and then with that light, to life. Not true. They are not informed about the reality. They are uninformed, too uninformed even to get disillusioned. In fact, a sensible disillusionment is good. It makes people think. Thinking changes the outlook and lays ways to progress. One of the causes of the backwardness of the countries that are poor, it appears, is the lack of disillusionments.

Education means another pair of eyes. We keep that pair open—wide open—often too wide to see anything correctly. Seeing correctly is important. To see correctly, we should see through eyes, not through books. We should see straight into the world, not via teachers. Books and teachers take away our real eyes, real nature, and real gifts. They blur our vision and disable our faculties. They don't promote the growth of our talents.

Education is just a measurement of what we are supposed to have learnt. Those trapped in the snare of the measured education become edgeless, and lose their fitness to cut in life. Those who sidestep or come out breaking the measured education get on. Those who study what is useful fare well.

Chapter 15

A Day with Dalia

One morning, sitting in his flower garden on a Teakwood chair under the hill station multistriped large umbrella, Hamilton was reading Dr Zhivago. At one place, he felt deeply moved and couldn't proceed further. He dropped the book, closed the eyes, and passed into a world of eerie emptiness.

While there, there seemed something touching his cheek. It was like the touch of his wife lost to cancer two years ago. Jack, his pet, would touch, but not so cautiously. It knows only to pierce. Jill, its mistress, is quietly lying on one of her sides leaving herself for her pups to suck. Renu, his maid, is too dignified to do this kind of a thing.

Hamilton's wife, the devoted believer in Christ, has perhaps come back alive, and touched him playfully. How can she come alive now? It will happen only at the second coming of Christ. If the dead people rise, then the living people must be transformed. Why Hamilton is not transformed? Who or what could have been good enough to show him so much love through that touch? He wanted to know. When he opened his eyes, it was Dalia leaning on his fur coat.

Dalia is his darling flower, always sweet to his heart. It was friendly with the wind, and they were pushing each other and playing between themselves. Obviously, they planned a fun and wanted to play it on Hamilton. Hamilton took Dalia tenderly and brought gently to his face. There, in that pink flower, were beauty and charm. He wondered and wondered at how rich it is with God's art. He wanted to watch more, find more, and wonder more. He wanted to take a plunge into each of its petals and through the stem pass down to the tip of its root and below. What is below the tip of the root? Earth. Down below? Hard earth. Below the hard earth? Rock. Below the rock? Harder rock. Still below, the hardest, what do we have beneath that? Fire, burning fire. Burning at the centre of our beloved globe. Not a small fire, but huge. Some call it as Lake of Fire, some Ocean of Fire. From when it is burning? It is not for the humans to know.

But Hamilton wants to know. What will tell? Who will tell? Which religion? Which scientist? Religions give one sentence statement. Scientists give a package of years. Not satisfying. Hamilton feels a vacuum. It is an uneasy vacuum. Who will fill that vacuum, and what will take away that uneasiness?

Again, Dalia touches his chin. Hamilton lays his eyes on her. She smiles. He smiles back. She keeps smiling. He also keeps smiling. Through that smile, they are passing into each other. Hamilton into Dalia, Dalia into Hamilton. Dalia is sitting in and into the earth, and growing in and into the sky. Hamilton is sitting on the Teakwood chair confined to the multicoloured umbrella.

Nothing separates Dalia from the creations of God. Hamilton is separated by an inner wear, middle wear, outer wear, and a fur coat. While inside the house, by the flooring tiles below, concrete roofing above and walls on four sides. Man is alone for all that surround him. Whereas for Dalia, everything that envelops her is her company, her strength, and her joy. Holding Dalia in hand, Hamilton wanted to speak to her. Understanding Hamilton's mind, Dalia said softly, 'Come speak, I would love to hear you.'

Hamilton wanted to give Dalia a kiss. Before that, Dalia gave him one. They were then engrossed in a conversation.

'Dalia, all flowers are beautiful, you, the most beautiful. All flowers look happy. You, the happiest. I envy you. You are more majestic than Catherine, the queen of Russia, and more blissful than a child in her mother's lap.'

'Really? Then why you are not so?'

'I couldn't find out why.'

'I have found out. Shall I tell you? Really?'

'Imm.'

You will not get angry if I tell?'

'I will not.'

'Sure?'

'Sure.'

'Okay. First of all, I should say, you are weak and your understanding is wrong. There is self-love, fear, and also—'

Before she said all she had to, ignoring the promise just made, Hamilton lost his cool. Didn't want to admit any of her remarks made about him, he bawled, 'Dalia, don't say like that. That makes me angry. Remember, you are right in my hand now. You will be dead in a minute if I crush.'

'Do, I am not afraid. When I am dead, I live. When I live, I am dead. I am both always. For me, life and death are the same. I just live since I don't know to do anything else. Others, whether good or bad, are not a problem for me. Nothing can threaten me. I don't know what fear is. When a volcano shows signs to erupt, I am least bothered. I feel as safe as ever. In fact, I would love it to erupt. If it erupts and discharges a river of glowing lava, nothing will happen to me. If it burns me up, nothing will happen to me. I will just turn into another form, ash. I would love to be ash also because the wind will spread me all over. That spreading will be a joy. I don't flee for life like you do. My readiness to die is my conquest of this world. That is why I am more queenly than your Catherine of Russia.'

Chapter 16

And His Wonderful Lamp

As of now, the road to education is operationally four-laned:

1) College lane
2) Correspondence lane
3) Political lane and
4) Bogus lane

Lane one:

Join a college, attend classes, read books, write exam, and pass.

Lane two:

Join a distance course, sit at home or roam, no books, only notes, read, or leave. Questions difficult? Write for answers the names of the pizza varieties you know. You pass.

Lane three:

Become a politician, take a power seat, say okay to a vice-chancellor, he arranges the highest a vice-chancellor can give you for free. Go black and black to the stage of the university centenary hall, and there wave a cheer to the crowd. You pass.

Lane four:

This is a lane of *Alladdin And His Wonderful Lamp.* Join no college, do no course, read no books, become no politician, add to your name just anything you like, even a PhD. You pass.

At the same time, if it is a medical degree that you annex in the Alladdin's style and want to practise on that, then you should take a long pause to review your decision. Otherwise, one day, you will blurt out the truth before the policeman. Then you will get into trouble. A serious trouble, rather.

Chapter 17

After Deducting

The origin of man is an unsolved mystery. In no country, human beings spring from the earth. They always come traveling down from somewhere, and settle. The nations to which the people came and settled early have got old. Some too old to stand upright without the economic crutches rented from the younger nations.

The younger nations are hale and healthy and economically energetic. How? Considerably, on the wealth looted from the old nations. India, we should remember, is one of the most looted nations. Just for looting some fellows invaded. And some who invaded despoiled the treasures and carried them away on horses and mules, ships and sailboats.

What shall we do? Is it too late to do anything about it now? Hamilton thinks it is not. We have been borrowing from our ex-looters and their successors who are in various parts of the world. It is puzzling if we are just borrowing, or we have any plan behind it. If we have a plan, what could that be? Possibly like paying the loan back after deducting what from them is historically due!

It will be wonderful if what has been borrowed from them as loans will be converted as aids, and further converted as dues adjusted against the loot. Then the account is settled. The age-long loot account.

India is not the only loot victim. The whole world, including Latin America, has been looted by the European expansionists. The looted nations have suffered an immense loss of wealth. In all fairness, they should retrieve it. How to retrieve? As an immediate step, they can form themselves into what they may call 'The All World League of Europe Looted Nations', headquarters at Cape Town.

In this matter, if India, which has been claiming to be the sole moral science headmaster to the world, could take the lead, without a second thought, all the loot-ravaged nations will readily join the league. The first to join will be South Africa, next will be Congo, and the third will be Botswana.

Chapter 18

Pure Loot

In the British days, an Indian professor coached up a boy who got a first class in economics honours. That honours helped the boy to become a clerk in the viceroy's office. Highly duty conscious, he was the model of honesty in keeping the records of how much we were being looted by the British. With that job so well done, the office was mighty pleased and named him Honest. He was sanctioned an annual increment of two rupees, and given promotions, one for one and half decades.

Upon the first promotion, Honest was trusted with greater loot files, which read like the thrillers of James Patterson. So much sensation! This sensation shook him to his marrow and fired his imagination. In imagination, taking History for a travel companion and interpreter, Honest set sail to the far-off lands.

First, he went to the sites of ancient civilization. There, he saw the defunct forts and sinking palaces, crumbling roofs and falling ramparts, shreds of pots and heaps of ashes, wind-swept bones and powdering skulls all around overgrown with bushes and groves laden with flowering creepers. Honest gazed at them long.

Then he made his way to the sites of recent civilization where human beings still live. There, he found rubbles of stonewalls, unmaintained palaces, half repaired structures, remasoned roofs, replaced tiles, rusted muskets, and cornered copper vessels. Nearby were unwieldy cannons and moss-coated cannon balls, spears, and wheel locks. Also, in addition to a heap of certain vengefully-shaped battle axes, was roofed shed lumbered with antiques and outlandish artifacts.

He strolled into the inner parts of the main palace where the paintings were peeling off for age and neglect. The stair hall was a sight of the king and queen used old time furniture, all kept for show.

Breath baited and voice stifled, Honest exclaimed, 'What are these, Mr History? Please tell. What?'

On a long drawn recollection, Mr. History broke his silence, 'All loots, nothing but loots. Loots of these greedy men looted from the weak and the meek. Look, many of these are yours. Straight on the inner wall hang the coats of arms of the warlike eastern kings. Here lies the throne of the golden peacock gathering dust. And there, a little away in the crown of a queen squints, your famed 108-carat Kohinoor Diamond.'

Chapter 19

Both Besides Adding its Own

When the Englishmen quit India, they didn't quit lock, stock, and barrel. They left so many of their unshiftable things with us. In their hustle, even their blood relations, they have jettisoned. Years later, many of their leftover dependents made an exodus to various parts of the world, especially to Australia. Those who didn't dislike this country stayed back and got absorbed into us as the happy members of our subcontinental family.

India is a sponge that can ingest anybody. For an interracial ingestion and bloodline fusion, it doesn't take longer. Half a century is enough.

The Indian ladies deserted by their British husbands are a forgiving kind. They raised no holler, rose in no revolt, made no representation to the United Nations Organisation to set up a commission to go into their grievances, and get a compensation from their run-away men. Instead, they chose to bear the wrong in their unexampled grace to suffer.

The British men who made haste to their native wives and their stepchildren left without settling anything with India. And we, for our part, let those troublesome men flee, holding back one thing—their language.

The power of the Englishman declined with time, while that of his language didn't. It grew. The empire that was political turned linguistic. Oddly, that linguistic empire also didn't survive. Not long after, it broke up. Now, each nation is linguistically also independent. It is developing its own English and own literature. America is developing American English with American English literature in the same manner as India is developing Indian English with Indian English literature.

For English now, there are two grammars: British grammar and American grammar. India is in a fix. It couldn't decide which to follow. In a state of disarray, it is following both besides adding its own. The same situation prevails in spelling. Computer recognises only the American English. On computer, you should be strictly an American. If you are any other national in grammar and spelling, it will bleed with red lines as far as you have gone the non-American way.

As things go, it won't be a surprise if both grammar and spelling get fully Americanized, and all nations adopt—including England.

Chapter 20

Despite Their M Tech

English teaches us that for a language to grow, it shouldn't block the entry of other languages into it. It should make friends with them, take and use their words unstintingly. Adoring mother tongue is nothing uncommon, but isolating it would end in retardation. Strict isolation will end in losing itself part by part. The first part to lose will be its speech.

English came as a crash flood and enveloped all nations. It is rolling the whole earth on the tip of its tongue. It is now the sole engine that hauls the professional world. In our country, the youngsters can be any empty in the knowledge of their mother tongue, but should be sound in English. If found unsound, they would be axed from the IT corridors despite their M Tech.

Chapter 21

Just a Happening

What is the beauty of English? Its worldly scope. It wins over the youngsters as a way to earn an income. The youngsters are after it. It amuses us to think that a good language is one that works as a means of good income. English is that for most of its learners. Where there is a shortfall in the yield of that income, it is made good by the diamond rich, the mineral rich, oil rich, and wine rich languages. What we note here is the charm of a language lies in its capacity to feed the needy. Not so much in its vocabulary or its literary heritage. Some of the languages, though classical, are materially not underpinning, with the result they have become either extinct or tongueless.

For one language to be able to bind all the people into a single linguistic bundle is unimaginable. For selecting English for the status it enjoys, nothing like a committee was formed. No country aired its views, none proposed, none seconded, none deliberated, none took a decision to put it into use. Nonetheless, it is there in the world reigning us all.

Had there been a committee to decide whether English should be accepted as the language for all world communication, what would have happened? A terrible war of languages would have broken out. England, as the archetype of the colonizing powers, would have dropped the first word bomb in the committee meeting. France, as a larger nation, would have cowed down England. Germany would have led a verbal expedition across the whole world excluding Russia. Spain would have fought tooth and nail against the proposal. China would have stoutly opposed fielding an argument that theirs, based on population, should be accepted as the international language number one, and English may take number two. For this row, there would've been no end.

How then English became the world language? Just a happening. Happening like how you and I have been made into what we are.

Chapter 22

Post-Graduation

Fifty years ago, post-graduation was the general culmination of college education. To finish that, one should spend one third of the Indian's lifetime. Post-graduate exam means condensing two decades of scholarship into a twenty-four hour report prepared in eight parts—the drafting time of each part being three hours. In a single attempt, eight parts at the rate of two for a working day. The last part done, you should wait.

After about two months' waiting, The Times of India would tell what you had meant to the board of examiners. If you had meant that you had agitated your case well on the answer sheets, everything is fine. Your university, your college, your teachers, your syllabus, your exam, and the newspaper. If you had meant otherwise, everything is bootless. Every play Shakespeare wrote, every song Wordsworth sang, every sermon Reverend Macphail gave, and every mantra the Holy Acharyas of Presidency chanted.

Chapter 23

Prof Bennet Albert

The scholars of Cambridge, Oxford, Montreal, and the Madras Universities taught Hamilton. Also, the products of Madras Christian College. The legend among those products was Prof Bennet Albert. There was depth in his understanding and clarity in teaching. Sharply critical, he could interpret and explain intricacies in a way easy for all to grasp. The way he dwelt on 'negative capability' that relates to John Keats is a proof to the kind of teacher he was. Though at times he would freeze his boys with his facial rigidity, he was not altogether cold. He had his own jokes, which he cracked one for every three months; annually, four.

We know during the monsoons, how it rains in the Indian east coastal belt. It batters with a fitful ferocity. In the rainwater, the college would stand knee-deep. Work would come to a standstill. The pious souls of the college would be fervently petitioning the rain God for mercy. But our Bennet Albert, cool with his steel determination, could be spied through the window wading across the red flood, eyes aiming pointedly at Hamilton's class. On landing, he would fill his hour with a lecture on Chaucer's, *The Prologue to the Canterbury Tales.*

It is a pure lecture, absolutely pure. No adulteration, nothing unrelated to Chaucer added. Not a word about the rain that had lashed and stopped, not a word about the spate that had raged and rested, not a word about the windstorm that had passed by, not a word about the trees uprooted. The thunder that rumbled and the lightening that flashed so close to him were, for him, something that never happened. All just an arrival staged, attendance marked, lesson handled, and leave taken. Now, that recollection is touching. Hamilton is moved emotionally.

Chapter 24

Secularism

In English, some words end with -ty. Some with –ion, and some with -ism. No -ism conveys anything clear-cut. All -isms are vague, vague generalisations. If a word ends with -ism, we can warrant that in it, there is surely something to foment trouble. These -isms are in religion in philosophy and in politics. Not in science.

There is no Daltonism, no Newtonism, no Einsteinism, no Ramanism, but certainly, we have Taoism, Asceticism. And Maoism. Also, of course, secularism. What is secularism? It is a word. Does it have any meaning? It does. What does it mean? It means using religion as a bulldozer not for crushing the necks or breaking the heads running it over the people of other faiths.

Chapter 25

The Great Astrology

Do we want our youngsters for ourselves? Yes. But how to stop them from bidding us bye-bye? This is a question we have been asking for half a century and over, but found no answer. Some say there is an answer. That great answer, astrology.

Some popular astrologers had told that a change of the name of the state capitals would usher in an era of prosperity. On this advice, the names of Madras, Bombay, Calcutta, and Bangalore have been changed respectively as Chennai, Mumbai, Kolkatta, and Bengaluru. It is these name changes, they contend, that is incidental to the growth of the movable prosperities we see on the roads now.

First, we had only state transports. No private transports, no family transports, no personal transports. Now the situation has changed. Just in a taluk, we can see in many four-member houses, for each member a four-wheeler parked. In dozens of baronial farmhouses, an Octavia; in hundreds of independent houses, a Honda City; in thousands of double-bedroom flats, a Hyundai Santro, iTen and iTen Grand. The roadside spaces mobbed with Tata

Indica, and the side gaps wedged with mini cars in the size of Nano. How now roadful of the wheeled prosperities that inch back and forth in cities, and speed past one another on expressways!

It is hoped that the future readers have started working on the remaining states. Bhopal and Patna are on the cards. We can't say when the renaming of the other state capitals will be resumed.

To resume is a little difficult. From which to start is a problem. The states are not identical. In area and population, they vary. Some in area are Goa, in population, Argentina. In which order the astrologers will advise the renaming is beyond our guess.

For the men with advanced sense of care, the future teller's clearance is a must. Without it, they will not initiate any move. So vital is astrology. So vital are astrologers.

Who are the astrologers? They are a class of extraordinary men. They can reveal the future. Reveal for all. If you pay them well, they will do well to tell you shortcuts to become so many things that you are not: famous like Barrack Obama, rich like Carlos Slim, and romantic like Silvio Berlusconi. They have prescriptions for instant transformation of women into their fancied celebrities like Britney Spears, Angelina Jolie, and Serena Williams.

The top future predictors are not easy to meet. They are at palaces and mansions. They were first with the kings and the queens. Now, they are with the presidents and the prime ministers. They were first with the princes and the princesses. Now, they are with the governors and the chief ministers. They were first with the aspirants to the throne. Now, they are with the aspirants to the parliament. They are busy people, always busy; busy with the study of where our luck hides, in which number, in which stone, and in which colour. They know what is good and what is bad, which is auspicious and which is not.

According to certain seers, the name of the existing capital of our nation also should need a change. Once changed, you know what they say? A great thing will happen. What? Our youngsters will forget the West.

Chapter 26

Delhi, Hot and Cold

Is there a country without a capital? No. Why? If there is no capital, where will the power gods congregate? And where will the people look for the fulfillment of the promises those gods have given? We have Delhi to look for.

Delhi is undoubtedly the best place for a capital. We all love it. We want to love it more, but we couldn't. The reason? Its climate.

The national capital is the political beehive. It is there the ruling bees meet to decide our destiny. For deciding the destiny rightly, the brain must work. For the brain to work, it should be sound. For it to be sound, the climate should cooperate. We know about the climate of Delhi. It is either stiflingly hot or bitingly cold. In summer, Dallol; in winter, Oymyakon. It is hard for the brain to be stable. In summer, it is molten. In winter, frozen. To contain the climatic horseplay is the focal bother of the bees at the central secretariat. Since the weather adjustment is the main business, office duty is just a side work done by the bees only when released from the heat or cold.

After a one-year stay at Delhi, anyone would find himself wishing the capital had been shifted to another place, a place where the climate is salubrious round the year.

So far, we have had capitals in several places, importantly in Calcutta and Delhi, and also in Daulatabad. The last is the choice of Muhammad bin Tughluq. The most unfortunate of the preys to the climate of Delhi, it is he who, of all the Indian rulers, had first comprehended the importance of a brain safe capital. If his choice had continued till date, we would have grown much faster and beaten many of the countries now economically in the front line.

Chapter 27

It Has to be Dark

Our economy is agriculture that is done on the land surface. Beneath the land surface, what lies, we don't know. Some say it is oil, but we don't dig it out. Our interest is to import oil from other countries, and sell it to the people raising its cost every time at midnight. Why at midnight? The midday is as good! Even better!

There must be something great about that timing, which the fortune tellers know. The fortune teller who timed midnight must be a great guy. He should be given a mega felicitation like it is given to the filmmakers, actors, actresses, singers, dancers, and comedians who provide us good time.

The astrologers entertain us no less. How much they plunge us in laugh! How many times the world has been destroyed, and how everytime it has re-emerged! We should thank the astrologers for all their forebodings that didn't happen. If they had happened, Hamilton would have missed himself half a dozen times. 1960 is the year in which, along with his earth, Hamilton for the first time disappeared. It happened at a midnight. Next morning, he reappeared with his earth, went to school, and wrote a test.

Poor astrologer! How much he would have bemoaned that his prediction had misfired! How much indignant he would have gotten with his astrology, and how much more with his neighbours, his family, and himself to see all alive.

To tell about our future, we have not only astrology. Also the other things like palmistry and numerology. What are these things actually? Are they arts or sciences? Whatever they are, these days, the people all over the world including the people of the superstition resistant nations like Albania, Bulgaria, and China want them. They are prepared to pay and believe, pay any amount, and believe anything.

The Election Commission of India comes hard upon the exit poll experts. The law forbids revealing the gender of the babies on the way to the world. Future foretelling is a taboo here.

What do the astrologers, palmists, and numerologists do? They also speak about the future. But how much we want them to speak! How much we want to hear! We never want a ban on them. Why? Because they are neither fully serious nor fully humorous, they are a mixture. From what they say, we know what to imagine as correct and wait for it to happen. If it happens, it goes to the credit of the astrologer. If it doesn't, it goes to the credit of astrology. And we know how to enjoy the joke of both.

Rather than the past, and even the present, we love the future the more because the past that dealt with us is gone. Of the present that is dealing with us, we know. About how the future will be, we are in dark. It is that darkness, which makes the future an attraction. For a thing to be an attraction, it seems beyond a point, it should be all dark.

Part Two

Chapter 28

We Go to Olympics

We, in our country, don't believe in wars. As a species interested to live, we believe only in defense. That means we will not be the first to squeeze the trigger. In not being the first, we have been notably consistent. Can any page of history show that we ever invaded England, France, Holland, Denmark, Portugal, or Greece?

Hit not first. Repulse if thrust. This is our military motto of yesterday, today, and forever. We return just what is served. Like us, if other countries are also resolved not to be the first to hit, there will then be no discord anywhere.

For us, peace is precious. That, we seek in all fields, including sports. That is why we go to Olympics. What for? To watch, only to watch, not to play, not to win a gold medal.

For us, to win and to lose are not different, just the same. When we lose a game, it is never a loss. We have earned a shining reputation for losing. That reputation we would never allow to wane. We are determined to see that it shines in every meet without fail.

Since our readiness to lose the Olympics is known, and well known, we go to the meet only to renew that readiness. We are not a kind to fuss if defeated.

When the foreigners launched attacks in the pre-independent times, did we fuss? Did we care to unite ourselves and chase them out? No. We wanted peace with them. How is the Olympics more important? We will be peaceful there also. That is why, unlike the gold, silver, and bronze mongers, we go to the Olympics just to try our luck.

The victory infatuates like America, China, Russia, England, and Australia strain a lot. They play and play, both boys and girls, taking part in all the events. They go mad with joy bagging cartloads of medals. But we would say what they have won are mere metal pieces. There is nothing to feel proud of. Do we ever feel proud that we have so much of gold, silver, and diamond hidden in the temples our kings have built? Who, born with a couple of legs, can trace those tunnels and chambers and tell their value?

The Olympic topper nations torture their players in the name of training and practise all the 4x12x30 or thirty-one days. We need no training, no practise. To feel happy that we have lost and the others have won, why so much training, and why so much practise?

Chapter 29

The Fighting Styles

Man does no work the same way always. His work style differs. It differs from time to time. The old style was employing the whole body, the recent style was applying the full arms.

Currently, work takes the minimum use of our body parts, even in warring. We want wars fought, how? Seated comfortably in the air-conditioned room of the army headquarters and fingering the panel board. Punch a button, bombs fly, missiles bounce, warheads scream, screech, howl, and explode. They fight in the air, on the ground, and over the sea.

Our effective soldiers are not the human soldiers. They are the chemicals packed in metal cases. Human soldiers are out of date, out of trend. Using human soldiers to kill human beings is unscientific. It will make us no war sense. Our present day society will not accept it as a decent war.

The countries have each an army as if it is a rule. Some have a huge armed force. You know what these army men are doing? They are doing nothing. The only thing they do is they keep themselves ready to fight, but not actually fighting. The army men, the navy men, and the air force men with their ultra modern terminators are doing a waiting. The marching soldiers, the sailing soldiers, and the flying soldiers are wasting their time. Wasting like the jobless civilians. The difference between the army men and the civil men is the army men are waiting their way to fight, and the civil men are fighting their way to bread.

The army men do a parade, eat, drink, and then we don't know what they do. They are highly fortunate, they are paid salary only to be ready to do their job, and pension for not even having started their work. It is so for the war men all the world over.

In the opinion of Hamilton, these men in fighting service in all countries can be sent back to their villages. There, they can dig lakes and canals, they can cultivate grains and vegetables, they can do cattle rearing for meat, dairy raising for milk, and poultry farming for egg. How useful these occupations are! But the countries are putting them on a wait till they lose their fitness to fight.

Why the countries are doing so? They want to tell the world how many of their men are in the army uniform, and how many they can spare for other nations if needed to keep peace. We know what peacekeeping is, and what the peacekeepers do while stationed in other countries. They behave like the schoolboys. Some worn from fighting yearn to get off. And when the chances to get off appear bleak, some, in despair, trigger into their own heads the rounds through the muffled nozzles of their handguns.

What do these mean? Mean one thing very clearly. What? The soldiers don't want to fight beyond a limit. The soldiers not wanting to fight beyond a limit is nothing new to history. We know the fate of certain aggressive grabbers of the other people's lands. Some of them were forsaken at the last minute. The war-weary soldiers slighting the authority of their boss, flung their arms in the air, broke loose, and fled home to have a sweet time in their choice club.

In the battlefield when his soldiers refuse to fight, what happens to the general? The general becomes a single man; and thereafter, naturally a philosopher. Philosopher on the principles of ahimsa, most enlightened next only to the great Jain Mahavira.

We know about the armed peacekeepers. They never brought peace—never. They left the field having sown seeds of conflict to grow with sharper thorns in varied forms. Those forms make a horrid account of woe.

How do they keep peace? It is by fighting. In other words, fighting is peacekeeping, and killing is peace keeping. When killing others is not possible, killing themselves is peace keeping.

Some countries, having driven the foreign army out, hand over the people to their native army. Some countries are experimenting with the types of government. They have not yet found out which is the best, the rule of the king, the rule of the dictator, the rule of the outsider, the rule of the army man, the rule of the people, or the rule of nobody.

Hamilton feels that a true democratic nation is the one that has no army. If we still have an army, still want to fight, and still keep the people trembling in war fright, we need not have, with all our wisdom, chosen people's governance. Now, the world is supposedly a democratic set up, largely, but not democratic enough to be able to pull on without firing a shot.

If the armament race, which the countries run, is run with the current vigor, one day, we, if we are alive to see, will see that democracy is worse than monarchy, even dictatorship. Monarchy and dictatorship in extirpating human beings were relatively less barbarous. Only democracy has developed weapons, the deadliest ever, and taken the world to the brink of total annihilation. For that annihilation to befall, what is now wanting is just a spark.

Chapter 30

Peace

In the place of despots and dictators, now the presidents and the prime ministers are fighting. People make some leaders, and after that, the leaders make the people their puppets. People give the leaders a taste of power, and after that, the leaders make the people the espousers of guns.

The men born and bred in a war environment would be war mad. There is a danger in installing such men on the democratic thrones. For the warmen to keep peace, gun and gunpowder are indispensable. The peace-loving civilians alone should head the nations. They only can set the world on a warless path.

When the general election of a country is near at hand, the views of the people of all nations regarding who should come to power should be gathered for world opinion. 95 per cent of the people would back the pro-peace candidate. Then what to do with the pro-war 5 per cent, only 5 per cent? Let them fight. Fight among themselves, die, and go to hell.

Chapter 31

The Money Sense

The poor people live on their little money they earn. Not until half a century back, the people had known that with more money, a better life could be lived. Now, the better life aspiration is slowly gaining ground. New breeds of the quick earners are cropping up.

What is earning? Earning means conversion of work into money. What is spending? Spending means conversion of money into pleasure. Hamilton feels that there should be a competition for spending. Then only there will be competition for earning. The people who have no taste for spending will have no taste for earning also. It was not given to all people of India to have a taste of more money. If they had, they would have adopted all possible ways to keep themselves economically strong.

Where people have been reduced to penury in their midst, surely there has been some grotesque philosophy at work under moral, social, and religious guises. The moral schooling is 'Contented life is the highest life'. The social discovery is 'Money is the root of all evils'. The religious instruction is 'Want a place in heaven? Become a pauper first.'

Living a natural life in a natural way is difficult. Against the natural human living, an umpteen number of influences have always been at work.

Unable to evade those influences, some people neither earn nor spend much, only save. Saving is a weak man's habit that takes us to a weak man's content. Only the contented people are poor. Contented people will not earn more, and will not spend more. Hamilton would say, 'Earning is personal and spending is national in effect.' When you earn, you build yourself. When you spend, you build your nation. Building his nation is everybody's duty. So build your nation by spending. If you have no money to spend, beg, borrow, or steal.

The poor countries that begged have progressed from begging to borrowing. When they reach the next stage, then all the countries will be rich. Stealing means not stealing literally. Doing it in the name of trading. What is trading? Trading is nothing but stealing with the concurrence of the stolen. Now, concurrence is necessary since open stealing has ended with the kings.

Chapter 32

At the Cross Road

Hamilton passed BA. It was not a small news. To hear that, the whole locality was elated. The distribution of sweets, the known mode of celebrating exams passed, took him half a day. The following week passed in exchange of a smile hitherto unsmiled. Then that smile began to irk Hamilton. He didn't know if to return it irked the neighbours too. In him was growing, at that time, a feeling he felt very uncomfortable with. He wanted to unload it, but found no way to. At last, opened a way, and that was to leave his place.

His parents read his mind and found all was not well with him. Yet, the light of pride on their face didn't dim. After all, passing BA in English Literature with a high grade, how great even if a fluke!

Hamilton's passing was his family triumph, but the air of triumph didn't endure long. It sank in the anxiety of what is going to be the next for the boy to do. The question of what he will do wriggled in most adult heads.

The neighbourly forecasts about his prospective plans roughly corresponded with his family's. The forecasts were:

1) To get married
2) To do business
3) To do law
4) To do masters or
5) To keep quiet

Hamilton felt like standing at a cross road. He had to think over each of the choices, and decide upon a course fairly soon. He began his analysis in the order in which the options opened upon him.

Chapter 33

Marriage

Marriage is one thing for which you can always yelp out a big no. You don't have to give reasons. For a man to marry, no age is old age. At seventy-five you can ask, 'What is urgent for that?' It may sound silly, but still, the bachelor's resistance to marriage is difficult to overcome.

Hamilton thought, 'I am between a man and a boy. More a boy. I have no age, no maturity, no job, and no earning. If I agree, it will be a nasty business altogether. I have a long way to go before letting marriage enter my head. Quite a long way.' His stand gained strength. The marriage threat receded.

Chapter 34

Business

Hamilton doing business! To think of it, the whole of his being reeled. He was not without his own view about what business is. His view was to make a living, business is a horror of a choice. He has heard the entrepreneurs vouchsafe that the business road is not a well-laid concrete highway. It has never been weatherproof. One lash of a loss is enough to wash it away, rendering it indistinguishable from the Sahara Desert.

To fare well on business, an inborn greed, edged with a lust for money is the first requisite. If you don't have that greed, and don't have that lust, better slash business off from your mind. It is a satanic route, too rough for soft angels to tread. No calling of this sort would suit a young man of the kind Hamilton is. Then, left with no way, but to come to terms with his view, business pulled its shutters down upon itself.

Chapter 35

Law

Hamilton doing law! To imagine himself as a lawyer, he felt he should laugh—laugh long loudly. Next minute, he felt he should weep—weep a lot silently. He knew to act as a lawyer and to act successfully, apart from his degree in law, he should have certain specific gifts. A good voice, a good confidence. a good politeness, a good laugh, a good muteness, a sudden flare-up, and above all, well timed submissions of your honour to the court.

The lawyers should keep updating their knowledge. The British day Indian lawyers were prompt in updating. They were voracious readers. The law sections and the top court rulings had been packed into their head to the breaking point. They personally carried a dictionary and a book of quotations to the court halls, or to the place of a dispute where they had a role to play.

Wren and Martin was to our lawyers what the authorised Bible was to the British. Our lawyers read Wren and Martin, but the British read no Bible. If they had read the middle part of the last chapter of the revelation, they wouldn't have shot their fellowmen and swallowed their belongings. It is the British who did the maximum of swallowing in the world. For swallowing in India came the governors general, and viceroys one after another, all Christians with the exception of just one.

To be the best Christian, according to the British, one should not be a Christian. They should do everything Christ was against. What were they, if not anti-Christians, in the days they suppressed India, Africa, China, and even America?

If the people of the west had read and understood the Bible, they would've just been minding their business in their own place. Leaving their horse rides, street fights, drunken brawls, coffee houses, dance halls, loved inns, night clubs, and musical operas, they sought to exemplify their greed in its worst form. They wanted the world. Especially India, Indian beasts, Indian birds, Indian fish.

The design of the British-built bungalows of the district collectors in India had been based on the western diet. In the design, an animal farm, a bird sanctuary, and a fish pond decidedly found a place. Soon on the departure of the British collectors, the farm, sanctuary, and pond also departed.

The British men liked India. The land area was so expansive. England is small. It is smaller than Germany, about half the size of France, quarter the size of Egypt. It is as small as a regional state of India. In width, it is another Andhra Pradesh; and in population, another Madhya Pradesh. In land spread, the then India was about sixteen times larger. In population, twenty times.

Here, they could fight any number of wars at the same time—so vast this land. And kill any number of people at the same time—so huge the population. They found the Indian army a herd of elephants carrying skinny men with stick spears, excellent for the British to have a good time using the shooting power of their guns and the killing power of their gunpowder.

They shot Indians brutally. In the process, they got likewise their own men also killed—one for every five Indians. It appears they had brought their own men over here to have them sacrificed as goats on the oriental soil of India. History doesn't report how many of their goats their world empire took to establish itself. Also, how many of their she-goats became widow goats. When the empire broke up, and its parts returned to their owners, the dead he-goats were just dead. Didn't return to their widow goats.

Chapter 36

Keep Quiet

Keeping quiet is not an easy choice, keeping quiet after graduation. Keeping quiet would mean literally one thing, but actually another. Not doing anything in the family sense is doing everything that daddy and mummy would order. What would they order? They have their stock eight commandments:

1) Get up early
2) Keep your room tidy
3) Don't give excuses for everything
4) Avoid going to Aunty's house
5) Bring the spanner set from Billy's workshop
6) Collect chit money from the farmland fat lady.
7) Read more and play less
8) Chat not too much with friends

Mother's indirect hints to Hamilton to marry Rita were slowly assuming a tone of open plea. That made him furious. He asked himself, 'Is not mom trying to drag me into the cotton dry land via that frail girl, her dream queen, for Hamilton? Will farming do any real good like putting the cotton farmers in a plane to enjoy a jet flight to Delhi or in a Plymouth car to do a cool drive to Kodaikanal? How many of the cotton farmers go coat and necktie in Vespa and give lectures on Milton? Once a farmer, always a farmer; the graduate farmer tills no different soil.'

Those into farming keep doing it for generations. They dwell in the same old house getting more and more weather worn, toiling on the same old dry land, getting more and more plough worn, and lead the same old life getting more and more time worn. They live the hard way, the hardness varying with the moods of clouds. They don't have the faintest idea of how to better their lot. They think suffering is honourable if they suffer in their birthplace. But those who couldn't think so are not here any longer. They are gone, those wakeful seeds. They are growing into mammoth oaks elsewhere.

Hamilton didn't have an attraction for rural occupations; least of all, for farming, though exalted greatly in his ethnic literature. The poets who glorified farming were not farmers. They knew no farming, and did no farming. Mostly idlers saddled with children in dozens.

To elude the threat to the dignity of education, he had to do something. The immediate was to break free from the cotton tentacle. Then told Hamilton, sitting up in a morning in the corner of his bedroom noiselessly, to himself, 'Out, out, you frog. Get out, leave this well, this little cotton pit. Be not a boy any further. Dare something manly. Flee to Madras, go to Marina, dive into the sea, dive deep. You will become a robust frog in the Bay of Bengal. There, you can croak in the all sea lingo—English. That will be pleasant, respectable, and remunerative.'

At this, all the options got knocked off, just with one remaining.

Chapter 37

Masters

Masters seemed a welcome option. The same foolish wisdom of his that went into the choice of BA English Literature, if opened, into MA English Literature also who, under the sun, can call Hamilton an ass. At the nucleus of that choice lies a job—some job—that he will get someday, somewhere, some way. How bloody important job is for man, though it is not a jot more than slaving under someone.

How funny it is to think that our life is job oriented, money oriented, slavery oriented. Each one has to inevitably do a job. Not doing is not slaving, not slaved, not liked. Not liked, not respected. People are respected according to where, according to how, and according to under whom they slave. Slaving on a job is not slavish. It is looked up on as an honoured status, universally honoured. Slaving is essential for man, essential for society. Not one will trust a man who is not slaving at all, however rich or scholarly he might be. An unslaving man should be careful, particularly in the matter of being happy. If he is found happier than the slaving ones, our society would get suspicious. It will expect him to make a good case for a probe, and if in the probe the case is found good enough, the society will expect him to soon end up in a police lock-up.

Chapter 38

English

The power of a language is heaven high. It determines the destiny of individuals, also nations. The Indian spiritual destiny is in Sanskrit, and material destiny, in English.

Outside England, English is one generation old. In the period of one generation, it has digested the native languages substantially. In five generations from now, it will complete digesting the balance. With that completing, people will have all forgotten their mother tongues.

At that time, English will not sound like English. It will get nasally intoned and shrivel into dashes of grunts. Man will then be too much into his headphone music to open his jaw wide enough to inhale a mouthful of air, and to blow it out in grunt forms. Grunt language will not work long. It will die down gradually.

We speak word for word, but that is in villages. In cities, people have given up speech. They interact look for look, stare for stare, shout for shout, growl for growl, snarl for snarl, and grumble for grumble.

As days pass, this wordless language will cease to exist. Action language will take over. Ours will then be a speaking body, the physical parts skilled in communication. What should happen between tongue and tongue on words will happen in India between hand and hand on sticks, in China between leg and leg on kicks, and in America between gun and gun on bullets.

In the academic world, English has been one of the most sought after arts subjects. It is not without a cause. For English, there is always a demand. Just by speaking it, a living can be made. To speak it professionally, we have places like the tutorial centres, reception counters, airway stations, and tourist sites. The scope of English has no limit. It is vast and varied. There are times it acts as a go-between and clears the blocks on the path of the young hearts. How warm feel the tourists from distant lands lured by the English of the Indian wooers on the sandy beaches of Kovalam and Eliot! How many of the gallants have, with their English, planted love in foreign women; and when it grew, settled wedded in Russia, Canada, and France! The magic of the language used by the author of Romeo and Juliet.

Chapter 39

Where to Join

In the field of higher education, the government men's colleges were among the first to come up. They were under the control and administration of the principals who maintained discipline at an illustrious level. In the course of time, things changed, extra academic interests and concerns crept into the minds of the students, and they indulged in acts, which were in the manner not very conducive to the quiet pursuit of study.

The government co-education colleges are slightly better. That can be seen from the attendance of the boys and the way they dress up. Instead of organising major disturbance, they sing the movie songs. They sing in the class when on session, in the office when it works, in the professor's room when he is in, and in the principal's chamber when he is out.

Here, the male percentage of pass may be anything. If low, to make that up are the girls. The girls of that time were not like these days. They were bookworms, they lacked the accomplishments the present day girls are formidable with, they hadn't known how to whistle a tune, climb a tree, fight a karate, club an impudent boy with a steel rod to bleed. Not one was in lipstick, in bob, or in super light minis.

The principals had to spend much of their time on resolving the crises the boys created by making unwelcome advances to the girls.

Presidency college is co-educational, but it is yet another government thing. Its only beauty is it has been staring at the Marina for centuries. In that college, the teachers were highly learned, but the students too, free. For the students, what to do for the day would depend on the resolution they would take just minutes before the classes begin. The resolution may be for or against attending classes, if against, they would turn away to Hotel Buhari for a tea, and from there, to Theater Casino for a show.

The women's colleges were good. They had been exemplary in their commitment to studies. They coached up and guided their girls individually. The university was pleased to award most of its first classes to these female scholars. But the trouble there is to take a seat and to study there one shouldn't be a boy.

Now where to join, in which college? Again, a cross road for Hamilton. His choice fell at last between two colleges: the Madras Presidency College and Madras Christian College. The Chidambaram Annamalai and Trichy St Joseph's never struck him. Why? They are not in the state capital. Who would like mastering from a place where there is no Mount Road, no marina beach, no lighthouse, and no Burma Bazaar? It will be fine doing it in a place, which is a sort of cosmopolitan youth club with enough of international student mingling. A foreign student is an information gramophone of his country. Set to play what a thrill? That student whether a boy or a girl is that country itself often found in bazaars. Whenever you smile at him or her, you feel you have traversed their country from one end to another.

After studies when you come back to Madras for a job, you will not be looked upon as an alien. You will be a Madras made and Madras equipped young man. Madras will like you firstly as its main product, and secondly as its multinational by-product.

It is necessary for us to have a definite idea of the college we want to choose. Hamilton had no idea, and couldn't pick one by himself, he was looking for someone to help. Then came one day a young man, an old student of Madras Christian College, bumping his head into Hamilton. He gave a perfect anatomy of that college showering at the same time lavish praises on it. That spelt the finality whereupon the cross road ceased to be a cross road. It became straight pointing Hamilton to Tambaram.

Chapter 40

At the Threshold

Hamilton wanted to see that college spoken high of by one of its old boys the other day. How to get there? To reach Madras Christian College from the city, 'Take an electric train that runs from Beach to Tambaram.' As counseled, Hamilton hastened to Mambalam Station, two streets down from his uncle's house at Lake View Road. In hand, the ticket bought at the counter, he crossed the bridge three steps a leap. On the platform was a huge turn out of people into whom he rammed about twenty feet. And there, he stood blinking.

The station was an ill-smell of tar mixed with the results of the uncontrolled human urgency. The people were tensed, as they know how tough boarding is. They were, as a block, moving front and back craning their necks to see if anything comes. Soon came what they were getting tensed for, and stopped abruptly. It was like an experienced, but a smaller version of a train with no engine.

In a second, Hamilton found himself inside a compartment caught up in the parcel of men and women sweating vaporously. Quite before the people's scrambling in and out was over, the driver sounded his horn and the train shook into a run. In half a minute, Hamilton was floating on the speeding ecstasy.

The train runs drawn by electric power on the overhead heavy-duty metal wire. It is not like the Delhi Madras Grand Trunk Express. Business like. Never cares if the passengers have all got in or not. Safety is out and out the lookout of the passengers. The train has responsibility to run only on the track, and stop at where it finds a station.

After the second station, Hamilton got a window seat. A real joy for a boy to feel the wind caressing his face, and to watch the furiously speeding train full length at bends. In half an hour, the shuttle reached the dead end, Tambaram. Hamilton got down. In ten seconds, the train should have become empty, but for the beachward crowd that rushed in like cattle.

The unloaded passengers hurried up all in the same direction toward the steel bridge. Fast and brisk, each one in the crowd was heading on in one's own haste. Some tumbled, some dashed. Those who dashed didn't say sorry, and those who were dashed didn't get angry. No time for all that. Slipping on the platform and hitting in the crowd are not a deal while on the way to workplace. For them, job was important, earning was important, life was important, so they ran and ran panting short of breath.

But where? Where exactly? Where would they go, and what would they do there? They were in the grip of fear, hearts thumping wildly, and chests heaving up and down. There appeared to be somebody not far away. Him, they feared—feared so much. What for they feared? Only those who feared know.

Some were couples hand-in-hand in frantic steps, racing. They didn't matter to themselves, but they mattered to somebody. The way they had learnt to matter to him was one of pity. This is the scene that Hamilton saw in all the stations the train had stopped. Hamilton, his certificates in hand and cash in pocket, paced up watching the plight of the urban and suburban railway India.

Upon the bridge, he was being swept on by the train mob just disgorged. The air was breezy. It fanned his sweat. Its touch was cool and mild. The air that was mild was not mild long. It suddenly blew hard and held him stiff. And then after a moment, it released him to fall. Luckily, his footing was firm. About the kind of act the wind had indulged in, Hamilton was not humoured.

As he walked, he lapsed into a trance. It was a benumbed few minutes of self-absorbed saunter. When he came back to his Tambaram sense, he had a doubt. 'How should I walk? What sort of gait would go fine with a fellow joining this great college?'

Again, the wind blew, and this time with more force. That, Hamilton didn't foresee. The others kept moving as though they were not in the least inconvenienced by what he thought was stormily buffeting. Then the wind calmed down. It was calm for a minute. Suddenly, ill-timed though, it turned frolicsome. Began shaping the attires of some women into domes and some others' into inverted umbrellas.

It did not rest at that. It was threatening to blow away the certificates, which Hamilton need not have brought. However, the certificates were doing him a good turn. They were guarding his identity besides affording him a right equal to those already studying. Holding his documents fast unto his chest, Hamilton sped on.

Chapter 41

The First Visit

Down from the bridge, now upon the road, the morning shining in the sun, Hamilton was feeling anxious to know where the college was. But he didn't like to enquire anyone. If he did, and if the fellows there were students, they might direct him by a shortcut to the air force station. Students are not the right guys to ask for ways.

Where a human gathering is likely, there, the tea stall would be the first to arrive. To serve at the college entrance had come Dhurga Bhavan. In it was running a smoky business on snacks and tea. The smell of the stall was tempting, but Hamilton didn't want to yield. Putting off his visit to the stall for better times, he kept his way.

Right in front, inside a compound wall, a luxuriant forest appeared. From among the trees, the college was showing itself in little parts. In one dart, Hamilton crossed the road and reached the gate. Through the forest on the walkway, he proceeded to the main block, head raised, and glances shooting inquisitively around. There were boys and girls aged from seventeen and above, boys in tight pant, and girls in sleeveless blouse standing in singles, in pairs, in small groups, in large groups, in groups of same or mixed genders, some appeared lively, and some sleepy. Some looking friendly, and some cross. Some smiling softly, and some exploding thunderously. Yet, all like good students each with a book in hand.

Here and there on the mud path margins were boys Chesterfield Blue King in their mouths, turning their heads away. No girl lit a cigarette or chimneyed out a whiff. This being his first visit, an advance visit of curiosity, Hamilton wished to go round and see the campus length and breadth. He went along whatever looked like a track passing past hall after hall, block after block, lane after lane, and tree after tree.

On either side were bushes thick and dense like in Amazon rainforest.

The sun was getting hotter. After a few minutes in what he thought was cricket ground sprawling like an island country, he turned back and came to the entrance of Heber, exhausted. A little in front was the water tank near which was where what he wanted was.

A bench. Hamilton slumped on that bench. Easeful on it which was clean, but for some scattered jasmines and bits of white paper, he gazed about. All green like the way to the Ooty Dolphin Nose. Upwards when he raised his gaze, it was a splendid sight of a dozen milk-white spoonbills flying in the sky westward over the trees.

Chapter 42

The All Round Messing

For children these days, home education starts at six months, and school education at two years. The child education commences with fun, which is later withdrawn. This withdrawal leaves a vacuum, but that vacuum doesn't remain a vacuum long. It is stuffed. Education stuffs the head. Environment stuffs the heart. The stuffing goes on and on and on. At the end, what had gone into the head and the heart make things a mess.

Watch the world. What is it if not a mess everywhere? But we are not appalled at the mess. Rather, we enjoy. Watching the high mess staged at times in various parts of the world, the remarks made by some critics are not palatable. They are blatantly caustic. They observe that all the inhabitants on the earth, compared to human beings, are more tolerant, more adjusting, more disciplined, and better behaved. They make a mess of nothing. The social manners of these species are full of love and understanding. There is order in their life and beauty in all they do. They are just wonderful, they are not taught the social behaviour that men are taught in schools, yet they practise the ideals that we could only preach.

It is man who messes up. What he didn't mess up? There is nothing he didn't. He messed up all. He messed up himself, his family, his society, his country, and the whole earth. Still, he is not satisfied. He wants to mess up more. For messing up more, in the world, there is not an unmessed square foot of land or cubic foot of water or air. But his messing nature hungers for new things to mess up. Those new things, he is locating in the sky. The mess has gone already to the moon. Now, it is going to Mars. Next from there, it will spread over to the other cosmic bodies including the sun.

Space tourism is expected to become real. When it becomes, the space will be many things that were not in the scheme of creation. It will go haywire. It will be found suspended with a variety of messing curios like space resorts, space hotels, space cottages, space cars, space taxies, space autos, space bikes, space cycles, and more.

With the space population swelling in the sky, it will turn into a space Madras with the space Cooums and space ditches. Due to the Cooums and ditches, the space will stink. And due to the traffics and transports, smoke will fill. Then the stink and the smoke will mix and suffuse the cosmos.

Result! Suffocated by the saturation of the stink and the smoke, may be as a fulfillment of Prophet Isaiah's prediction, 'The stars and the constellations shall not give light, the sun shall be darkened, and the moon not shine.'

Chapter 43

Five Decades Back

Hamilton was staying with his uncle, his mother's youngest brother, a revenue official. His house at West Mambalam was Hamilton's base for launching himself into a college to do his post-graduation at Madras.

At that time, Madras was not like how it is today. The residential parts were mortar built and hoary looking. The tiled buildings were everywhere in the city including the sides of the Mount Road. The tiles were mini-sized, semi-circular pieces inserted head into tail and tail into head. The conversion of the tiled roofs into concrete tops had just begun. Anna Nagar had been partly born and K. K. Nagar, in the prenatal making.

Like now, the Madras winter was not far different from its summer. It was brief, too brief to take away the heat charged by the rest of the year. Annually, it was nine months of African summer and three months of Asian summer that baked us in sweat and fried us in heat. The coldest day was hardly cold. The lament of the lovers of the real cold was they always missed it at Madras.

The sightseeing tourists of those days, we should say, were not fortunate. They missed what the people in thousands enjoy today. The eye-catching monumental squares on the seashore were not there. In their place was an arid stretch of wavy sand dune.

We know, in India, sometimes it rains. In those days, when it rained at Madras, it did for the good of the people. Buried no apartment, rolled no house, shoved no hut, blew off no thatched roof, felled no tree, and took no toll of life.

Nature was kind, the sea, calm, and the waves of Marina playful and visitor-friendly. We never heard them drag the hapless boys into water and twirl them cruelly to death.

Madras, known for a number of wonders, is most widely known for the River Cooum that stinks. In those days, its stink was just typical of a river, not gruesome as now. Crossing it in a handrickshaw without corking the nose with a hanky was then not impossible.

City buses were there, most of them unclean. Some outside, dusty; and inside, dirty. Reddish, no bus was shapely. Their bodies had been bent and dented. In the starting shake, the sides dropped plate by plate. The roofs of some were rust eaten holes in rain like a sieve letting all the water inside.

The peak hour buses staggered on the road, slanting for the load of the boys squeezing on the footboard, and dangling from the window bars. No bus ran fast. They roared their way like an old lion ailing from an awful sore throat. Drunken driving and road accidents were there, but seldom killing any. Many of the bus stands were also the bus depots. The star hotels were yet to come up. Building craze hadn't yet maddened the flat promoters. High-rise buildings were rare. In height and grandeur, the LIC was the queen of Mount Road.

There was then a shopping complex called the Moore Market built in bricks by the British. It was abutting the Madras Central Station. Not huge in size, but seductive in beauty. There is not another like it anywhere. But now it is gone.

The Southern Railways brought it down in one pull, and swallowed it overnight. That swallowing was mourned with a great grief by the whole city. The aesthetic wound left by its mortality would never heal. Never for those like Hamilton who had loved it with their weekly visits. In its place, now stands a wing of the Central Station, the terminal of the short route trains.

Beauty is quitting Madras. It is quitting one by one. First quit the natural beauty, then the Pallava beauty, then the Moghul beauty, and then the British beauty. The present Mount Road beauty, the Bharat Insurance Building, is posing a threat of leaving us. The debilitated parts of the Indo-Saracenic Central Station, Egmore Station, Royapuram Station, Madras University, Anna University, Chepauk Palace, General Post Office, King's Institute, Government Museum, and certain other structures like Victoria Public Hall may at any time fall to the dig of Volvo L120 E. For the lovers of the Madras architecture, now is the time of anguish.

The Madras people loved the city with all its attractions. But their insatiable attraction was cinema. The theaters were full and in weekends, crammed. But the cramming didn't last long. The movie fans were kept glued all the time to the sofas by the television sets at home. The theaters fell thin. Some were closed, some disappeared. Those that disappeared were undergoing some metamorphosis behind a steel curtain. After a time, when the curtain was taken off, they reappeared. When they reappeared, they were in another get up as shopping plazas prismatically lit and pleasantly cooled.

On the city roads, all turns were U-turns. The signal points were not many, roads were narrow, there was no timer, no central median, buses were few, autos half as many, Fiats and Ambassadors were black. If taxies, the same as now, tops yellow and sides black. No call taxi, no share taxi, all the light vehicles ran on petrol for one rupee a litre.

Madras had decades to go to become a Detroit, and when it did, it became undiscoverable. The city suffered excavations, subways, and tunnels slitting it criss-cross. The roads are already circus tents, on the arched flyovers the vehicles playing bars. The throbbing stream of the Indian two-wheelers make a bewildering assortment of numberless brands. The city main roads are the automobile rivers all day running full.

The western four-wheelers like Baby Austin, Bentley Morgon, Morris Minor, and Rolls Royce honking their horns of pops and bass can't be spotted on roads. The western two-wheelers like Norton Commando, Bonneville, Vincent Black Shadow, Matchless Silver Hawk, Triumph Trident, and Rock Hunter have gone missing.

No lady rode a bike. Only the boldest sat on her husband's Enfield, eyes shut, and arms clamped to his waist. The pedestrians took a leisurely cut where they pleased. Mount Road could be walked across by the oldest man of Madras at any unhurried pace of his.

The traffic flow was smooth and unvarying. It was never diverted except for the visits of the real leaders like Nehru.

Hamilton is not sure whether the power vehicles were red-lighted then. Since all protocols that we adopt are the continuation from the British, we can presume that the red lights should have flashed on the roads, though not in number so many as now. For us, it is a confusion. Why, of all colours, the red has come into use? Red doesn't go well with our sentiments. It stands for things like blood, violence, and danger. People want not blood, not violence, not danger. They want to drive, if possible, freely; if also possible, happily. The red-lighted things are aberrant, meddlesome, and high-handed. They force their way out of turn to the burning displeasure of the people who drive paying the road tax.

However, for our own good, for priority overtaking, we must allow three exceptions: one, the police van blaring its way to disperse an unruly crowd; two, the fire engine pressing its way to spray out a blaze; three, the ambulance yowling its way on a life saving rush.

For those driving on business or pleasure, time management is their personal lookout. It is wrong to steal into the space of others and bawl out for clearance with a show of fist. The security to the important persons is not in the red bulb, not in the fierce bawl, not in the threatening fist. It is in the advance containing of causes of insecurity. Had that been understood, India wouldn't have lost the three of its top lives—two male and one female.

Chapter 44

Car Starts

In those days, driving a car was not difficult, but starting it was. So many times the key should be turned. For each turn, there would be an empty whimper. The starting would occur on a chance ignition. Most cars were key started, some push started, and some rod started. Push starting is a standby for key starting. Rod starting is a standby for push starting. Push starting is for tests. Only the workshop boys do it for a jump-start. Rod starting is no more in vogue. It vacated India four decades ago.

Among the starting varieties, rod starting is the most sensational. To know what it is, take a clue. It is like starting the mini-generator. In the place of the rope, there is a rod. Put that rod in the nose of the engine. Turn it clockwise hard—turn and turn. Hard again. It suddenly catches up. It means the engine has agreed to work, the first successful step for the vehicle to move.

Driving had one more meaning—fun. Nobody can foretell if a vehicle would surely reach to go where it was started. The early automobile technology was such that vehicles of even some great world leaders pre-closed their journey and were towed away.

For long journeys, the motor vehicles were generally not dependable. Every part was a problem. The worst was the radiator. From it, water would evaporate, the engine would get red hot, and spew out black smoke. For emergency watering, the wayside lakes were relied on.

The next trouble was the spark pluck. Once oil enters, the vehicle would limp, shake a few times, then stop dead. So long as the vehicle runs, it is a pleasure. The moment it stops, it is not. Then? It is an adventure. The nature of the adventure would be determined by the place where, and the time when the vehicle would breakdown. A midnight breakdown on a desolate highway would be the most adventurous.

Air brakes, coolants, and air conditioners were not there. Of the three, the air conditioner was the last to come. When it came, it came not straight to the car. It first went to the residences of the upper class men, then to the rooms of the hotels they stayed, and the clubs and hospitals they visited. Then came to the houses of the upper middle class men then to cinema houses then to shops then to the express trains before going to luxury buses. And it came finally to the car.

In India, cars were first with the Angles then with Anglo-Indians, and then with who were neither. When they came to Indians, they came first to the kings who were multi-womened. Matrimonially, they were eastern; romantically, western. Egged on by their western ladies, they imported the best of the western luxury vehicles.

India, we know, is no way like any of the countries in Europe. The Indian climate and the Indian lifestyle were least agreeable to those ladies. The Indian kings didn't match their taste. The Indian drivers with their turbulent driving and the rugged roads, and with their serpentine bends didn't suit the imported vehicles. The imported women and the imported vehicles felt ill at ease on the Indian scene. So the kings could trust neither these dames nor these cars, as they were always ready to run—run back to the place of their make.

On weekends, the Anglo-Indians would push their vehicles out from their garage. Park in front of their bungalows and start their repairs. In every street, at least one could be found lying under the engine and downing some part. His cherubic little daughter would keep standing with a jar of water for her dad to drink. Then from underneath the chassis, he would reach his hand over. Clasping the jar, in a single gulp, devour the content. When he is done, he would return the jar releasing a gasp monstrous like his engine at the first turn of the key.

At that time the Anglo-Indians were fair in complexion, men were tall, women were cute, the men wore pants, women wore skirts. Their look was curious, especially their eyes. For the Indian women, the Anglo-Indian females were a critical picture of incompleteness. For the Indian men, they were the noteworthy, life-size dolls. Whatever the work they did, inside the house or outside, for doing it better, they got into a dress special for that work.

Men covered their whole body, their women didn't. They left out the legs below their knees. Their male style drew the local men into pants, but their female style didn't work on women. The native women loved their mile-long saree too much to take on the western blankness of the lower legs.

Chapter 45

The Chain Snatching

In India, in those days, the poor people paid no attention to their dress. Few were in full dress, some in half, some in quarter, most in much less. The middle class men dressed in white. They flaunted the fabulous shirt for upper covering and the cotton cut piece for the lower.

The rich men dressed pompously like the palace advisors, turban on head and umbrella in hand as if it always rained. They fastened the gold-embroidered towel one circle round their neck with the ends hanging on their chest, and bandaged their legs with silver-lined dhotis. To adorn their feet, they wore the alligator-snouted shoes. When their women dressed, they did it with half their weight in gold, quarter in silver, and the rest in silk. Their ornaments thrice outsized their figures already buxom. The gold, silver, and diamond meant to report their social size were displayed over their bodies on the select visible parts. Gold attracts all, but the attraction it exercises on women is intense.

Next to women, its intensity falls on thieves. Gold theft began the day the first bit of gold ore saw the light. It grew with the growth of the gold mines and the multiplication of the women fond of jewels. Now, the theft goes on all roads, all lanes, and all places.

The bike sort of gold snatching is the recent addition to road thievery. It seems it has been added after a series of field tests. In the operation chain gold, the operator's instant escape is the most important. For that, an appropriate vehicle is essential. The elusion of the chain cutter is in the swiftness of the vehicle he uses. Formerly, such a vehicle was not there.

Bicycle, though made in England, was leg-pedaled and slow. Before wheeling ten feet on a small cry, the public would rush up and grab the thief by his throat. Enfield, sturdy, but it would not start for a single kick. If started would be treacherously noisy. It wouldn't cooperate for a vanishing that has to be played like lightning. Ambassador, though hefty, after reaping a gold piece from a woman's neck to reach a disappearance in a second, it will not help. The plate number can be noted from a distance of two kilometres. Foreign vehicles were good, but only for family outing. Professional vehicle, good enough for this super fast action, had not been thought of yet.

The erstwhile vehicle makers were too commercial. They had not taken the jobless youths into account. Now, it is not so. The manufacturers have diversified their make. They meet the self-employment requirements of the youths to the maximum. Nowadays, on roads, any speeding two-wheeler can be one of a chain puller.

According to the seasoned professionals, the gold-cutting career is not a fool's choice. It pays. One kick of the starter, one pull of the chain, one turn of the throttle, in one minute out of sight. And in hand, minimum one lakh rupees earned in two minutes. No tax.

The chain plucking enterprise is a one-time investment. And that is on the bike to buy, which the banks assist liberally. Apprenticeship is no problem. It can be finished making off with a two-wheeler found without locking on the way to the Crocodile Park. The youngsters, who have realised its scope, don't miss this opportunity, which is literally golden.

Most employees in this line are arts, science, and engineering graduates. Because of their sound education, this industry has vastly grown. Its growth is the fastest in cities. Next comes the towns. For villages to pick up, it needs time. To do villages, the locals don't dare. The executives have to come from far away places.

Chapter 46

The Filling

In the city of Madras, filling of the land with buildings is the fastest of the business races. Every piece of land is turning into a structure, mostly massive. In the gaps between the road and the line of houses, erections pop up. For this, there is no stopping. Of course, there are laws to stop—paper laws. Also, laws to permit. Field laws. Under the generous winks of the latter, the land filling is going on in the fullest swing.

There is another filling. Human. The industrialists coming from the east and the west, the businessmen coming from all corners of India, the jobless coming in search of jobs, the youngsters coming for schools and colleges, the construction workers coming from Bihar and Manipur, the criminals coming for hiding, the pickpockets coming to buses and bazaars, the burglars coming to break the ATM, the musclemen coming to play stunt roles in cinemas, the train urchins coming for cleaning the hotels.

The man-woman pairs coming to see the city, the fair girls coming for film chances, the smart women coming to set up beauty parlours, the nomadic women coming to sell needles and fox teeth.

In summer, the tender coconut men; in winter, the Nepalese woolen women, the roadside vendors, and hawkers. All of them in the bazaars calling their ware and killing our Tamil.

The train and busloads of shoppers who commence their visits at sunrise, stay on till after the day is done. This is the filling of floating kind.

The buffaloes have vacated the metro part, but in their places are the boys who throw the milk packets that burst on our doors. These packets, along with the carry bags, go into the corporation lorries. From those lorries, the packets and the bags fly up and spill over our heads. From our heads, the Marina breeze sweeps and leaves them in heaps. This is the filling of the flying kind.

Then come the ever increasing road wheelers. The discharging of their half burnt petrol and half burnt diesel envenom the air. This is the filling of the envenomed air.

The filling of buildings, of motor vehicles, of men, of women, of boys, of girls, of polythene waste, of kitchen garbage, envenomed air, leaking sewage, unsanitary slums, unclean ditches, the unsightly daybreak railway borders, and everything else make our city a stink, a horrible stink. Indoor and outdoor both are a sweat and suffocation.

For all these, Madras is not disliked. It is loved, being loved, and loved; visited, being visited, and visited; and filled, being filled, and filled as one of the most admired state capitals of India.

Chapter 47

Ms Universe

Madras is celebrated for very many great things, but all those things didn't please Hamilton. What pleased him was a man at the university. There, at the reception, was he—warm and happy, beaming with a smile always. A cap on head, he was not young. Side hairs had started to grey. Him, Hamilton loved and met, met often. He said things, rather thought aloud, many of which Hamilton hadn't heard before or since. They were about Madras, about the university, about the teachers, about the students, and about the hostel boys and hostel girls given over to the city style of indulging in the pleasures of their youth.

Whenever Hamilton met, he found in him a friend. He is one person who needed no joke to rock with a laugh, no stimulant for his goodness to flow. Such a man! Hamilton thought he should separate his spirit abstract—if there is a way to do so—take it home, call out his uncle, and tell, 'Look here, Uncle. This is Mr Madras, Hamilton's Mr Madras whom every one should meet at least once in his lifetime.'

To select Mr Madras, shows are held at the government stadium. But all don't go there to watch.

Those who go know how the contestants look and what they do. Grim-faced, bony-cheeked, hollow-stomached, and overstrung muscles worked into bulges of lumps and knobs. When they show their bare bodies, wringing and stretching the arms this way and that, how is it all? You must see it for yourself. They are the ones who bag that title, Mr Madras.

Demonstration of masculinity is conducted as a public show, but the demonstration of femininity is not. In the Miss way of selection, women are enjoying an edge over men. In the news, we see Ms City, Ms State, Ms Country, Ms World, and Ms Universe. But men, we miss. No gradewise male selections now.

Instead of holding separately, these contests can be held for men and women at the same place and at the same time and their results announced side by side. What a grand affair it would be if a wedding is got up for Mr Universe and Ms Universe at Morgan Plaza, the Seven Star Hotel, Beijing, China! How nice it would be if we are invited for that wedding reception. What a soul-melting time we would have if in that reception, that ravishing young Chinese artist in her honey-like accent sings that A. R. Rahman's *Chinna Chinna Aasai.*

But . . . but . . . but the trouble with the Mr Universe and the Ms Universe is they neither see each other nor fall in love.

Chapter 48

The Madras Cleverness

Hamilton thought Madras must be a city of gentlemen. He wondered if the receptionist could be so good and so fine, how good and how fine could the vice-chancellor be with his gilded turban on his famous medical head. The clever men always fix something on their heads. Yet, all clever men are not good men. Some are bad, some are very bad, some thoroughly rotten. A man in the guise of a railway porter, with a piece of pink ribbon pinned to his tuft, took away a luggage and vanished into the crowd. The loser lady blew out her lungs screaming, 'Oh, my handbag! My house key! My cell phone! My passport! My ATM card!'

This happened last week at the Madras Central Station. On this rotten side of cleverness, there are advanced kinds too. They are common in business, also in government.

Madras is a place of unbeatable cleverness. You may ask how this cleverness came. It is not self-acquired, it is an inheritance. It is an inheritance from the early foreigners who were tireless hunters of pleasure. They didn't like doing works; they got them done through the men of this place. The men of this place did them all sorts of works from cutting the wood to cooking the food. Leaving such works to the local men, the foreigners enjoyed the best this place had.

As needs hardly be told, they came to India mostly to enjoy—to enjoy the pleasures their countries were short of. To win those pleasures, they adopted four ways. First, talk; second, threat; third, assault; fourth, seizure.

If they desire a thing, they would first start a talk. If talks fail, they would threaten. If threats fail, they would assault. If assaults also fail, they would seize it and walk away. This method, our native men watched, liked and followed, and they still follow. Those who follow it cleverly are now the owners of the city.

The city people are not native of this place, they are outsiders. Their native places are away and far away. They may be any district, any state, any country, any world, any planet, or any universe. Here at Madras, nobody is a friend, and nobody, a foe. None to love and none to be loved, none to trust and none to be trusted. All have come, to begin with, in search of a living and then to grow on whatever later comes to them handy.

For anything you have or anything you can do, there is always a demand in the city, anything. You have to just use it. If you have learnt the art of using, you will soon reach such a great height that you will wonder at yourself, 'Is this me?'

After arriving at Madras, the only thing that has to happen to you is to get rich. Madras enriches all, some slowly, some very slowly, some fast, some very fast. To get rich the fastest, one should be the crookest.

The Madras people don't see much into others. They don't speak much or hear much. They have limits to everything. Yet, they live together since it is a tolerant city of adjusting outsiders. It is good that it is from outside they have come. If they had all taken their origin here, Madras would not have become the hi-tech city that it is. It would have been an insignificant fishing village like it was before the times of the great Naiks.

Chapter 49

Admired and Wondered

The world is full of greedy people. Of them, the greediest are the richest. What for people become rich? Not just to make the ends meet, to meet the basic needs small money will do. Then why they become rich and why so rich?

It is to be heard as rich, to be seen as rich, to be admired as rich, and to be wondered as rich. At the level of being heard, seen, admired, and wondered, there are already some in India. But they are not enjoying them proportionate to their riches.

In villages, richness is respected—these days at least to some extent. But in cities, it is not. The city men know how the rich men became rich. The rich, therefore, are a sport to laugh at. To be laughed at, the sensitive rich feel demeaned. Poor rich men! They are trying hard to rebuild their respectability.

There are some rich men who want to be more than wondered, want to be worshipped. There had been some such in the world. You know what they did when their appeal for worship was turned down? They became bad, very bad, even murderous.

The first rich man who begged the people for their worship, and when it was rebuffed by some in shame, put them to death, was Nebuchadnezzar. Who is this man? He is a king, a great king. It is he who raised one of the wonders of the world—the hanging garden of Babylon.

Chapter 50

Honeyed Flatteries

Income is not always a pleasure. For that, there is a side of pain also. If you earn an income, you should pay a tax. That tax is a recurring nightmare, an annual plunder that the government mounts on earners. The tax-harassed are in a hell, they are looking for someone to redeem, but who is there to? None. But if the government wills, there is redemption.

Why not an idea like the government giving a choice to the tax trounced big shots to write a book highlighting how they became rich? For the honest expositions, the authors can be exempt from tax liability for life. If exemption announced, the creativity of these rich men would bring out new epics. New epic heroes and new epic heroines would emerge in a large number, from rags to riches sort, from streets to airports type, and from den of vices to sainthood kind.

Confessing the secret of how they became rich will be delicate, surely delicate. But judge it from its motivational worth, a work that is confessional is bound to be inspirational. Each one of such works will raise a thousand men, say, through honeyed flatteries, deceitful frauds, criminal shadiness, daring exploits, Machiavellian inventions, and the like. Without the help of these techniques, nobody becomes truly rich.

Chapter 51

Terrorism -1

Time runs nonstop. To measure it, there are units. The unit to measure a hundred years is century. Each century is special for something. The current one is special for what? It is special for terrorism.

What is terrorism? We don't want a vague definition. We want a definition with a good explanatory note, which would drive its meaning home into us. Where to get it? Hamilton says we don't have to look for elsewhere. The terrorists themselves have come all the way down and explained clearly.

First, it was explained to us at our national capital, there at our parliament, the top power centre, brain centre, muscle centre, and the centre of all for which crores and crores of us look for solutions. Now, for all its security tightness, certain armed strangers steal in and take the house by storm. Kill twelve and injure eighteen. This inhuman act of storming, killing, and injuring are what we call in one word, terrorism. One explanation, given to those who should know its meaning first.

Do you want another? Another explanation was given to us at our business capital, there at our top beauty centre, fashion centre, glamour centre, money centre, a centre that grants every desire man has. In that great city where the most affluent live, we, the people, heard those heartbreaking gunshots, blood curdling bomb blasts, and watched the conflagration that raged in that hotel for days. And the report we got had noted that the killed were a hundred and sixty, and injured over three hundred.

Another explanation given to those who should know its meaning next; first, explanation given to the centre of our overall policy and administrative regulations, and the next given to the centre of our trade and enterprises.

Ultimately, from these explanations, what we, the people of this great nation, should learn? And what we should do? To learn, there are so many lessons that we can't enumerate, but to do there is only one. Listening. Listen to the God made cosmos from the unscaled height of which a scary warning blares:

'Your attention, please, in whichever part of your country you Indians may live and whatever the security your government promise. First, insure your life if it is still with you, and then insure your hut if it is still safe. Don't be careless like the Bombay guests and their hosts were.'

Not a day passes without a terror column in the newspapers. Terror incidents are such a recurrent happening. But what happens everyday ceases to be a news. It is something we read, get hot, get cooled, and then forget. We have got that much used to the terror shocks. Hereafter for us, it will not matter whether terrorism is there or not.

Chapter 52

Knows Only to Carry

Man, in his life, manages many things, but managing a human being is hard. Managing an animal, harder still. Managing to sit on its back and to gallop, quite an exploit.

The kings must have been real great fellows, their sons and daughters too. They have not only ridden horses, sitting on their back without falling, also bouncing forward in full armoury, have fought. Fighting a battle is not like playing ping-pong. It is quelling human wolves rushing in to tear to pieces.

Fighting a horse war must have been a great spectacle. Horses standing on the hind legs and neighing, swords of the horsemen clashing and clanging, the injured men crashing and rolling, the fierce horses fretting and chafing, the gun chaps firing shots, and the confused captain outroaring the din. It must have been a terrific sight. The sight of killing and getting killed. That hot while of the battle rage, the horses must have enjoyed more than their riders.

The war horses are more than mere quadrupeds. They are man's executive colleagues—battlemates. Dauntless and unyielding, the horse is an intelligent and integral part of man's war action. Man killed and the horse carried the killer braving all risks. Thus, kingdoms were won.

Conquests of kingdoms are the results of the joint endeavor of the horse and the horseman. Logically, the horse has equal right to the throne. The horse and horseman should rule jointly, or cut the kingdom in half and horse should rule a part; but the poor foolish things, the horses, like the slaves in the past, just carried their masters. Didn't claim their due.

Chapter 53

Your Unknown History

The history of your country is not about the kings and queens who ruled. It is out and out about yourself. It is your biography. Your name is there in full book at each page, each sentence, it is with your initials, address, pin code, also with the factual reference to your ancestral past. As it is your story written with somebody else as its hero, it is vital that you read it.

In the course of history, you are not on the side of your nation. You are on the side of the invader of your nation, the attacker of your nation, the oppressor of your nation, and the killer of your nation.

Sometimes you are close by his side, sometimes very close to him, sometimes you are inside him, and sometimes deep inside too. But you have not seen him. Why? Because you have not seen yourself first. You are invisible, invisible not only to others, but also to yourself. Why invisible? You don't see how you should.

Alexander invaded. You are there close by the side of Alexander. Where? You are where you didn't invade Macedonia. Vasco da Gama attacked. You are very close by the side of Vasco da Gama. Where? You are where you didn't attack Portugal. Duplex oppressed.

You are inside Duplex. Where? You are where you did not oppress France. You are deep inside the killer of your nation. Where? You are where you did not seize General Dyer's gun and shoot him without a word of warning and kill him heartlessly.

You means everyone on the invaded side of the nation, the attacked side of the nation, the oppressed side of the nation, and the killed side of the nation with his ancestry and posterity.

There is no history independent of people. There is no history without people's cooperation. You are the maker of your country's history through someone you allowed to overpower and rule. The ruler is the molder, and you are his finished product. You are what you are because the ruler was what he was. What are you? You are what the ruler wanted you to be, or what the ruler didn't mind your being what you are. The ruler followed his will, and you, his word. He ruled you. And you were ruled.

The ruler knows you every molecule. But about him, you know nothing. You are ignorant. The cause of your ignorance may be your nation, your religion, your society, your family, or yourself.

Whatever the cause, now you should know both the ruler and yourself, his mind and your mind. If you know from the depth of that knowing, a new light will shine. That is the revealing light. That will reveal a million truths not revealed so far.

If that light doesn't shine, something is wrong with you. Damn yourself, you are a historical miscarriage. Though born, you are misborn. Though lived, you have mislived. You are a man who has misspent his life, you have missed yourself somewhere in the darkness of your past, you do not know who you are, what you are, and where you are. You don't know your real name and real address, though all these are there in the school certificate, census manual, electoral role, ration booklet, and the Aadhaar card issued recently.

The ageless universe with all its size, the huge world with all its wealth, centuries of rule, alien and native, and the responses of your patriarchs; and you have built you up bit by bit and brought you over where you are. That place is your place, and you think for this life you deserve only that.

Our thinking is a misled thinking. Misled by those already misled. We don't think what we think, we have been made to think the way we think. All of us are happy that we are known as what we are, but you are not you.

You are what someone had told. If someone else had told something else about you, you would have been not you. You would have been someone else—another you.

A man at last is one who has not seen himself. He is not more than just the reports he has received about himself from certain people accidentally. He is a photo framed and mounted on the wall. Away from that wall and outside that frame, he is a stranger. He can't recognise himself.

Chapter 54

Selection

For Hamilton Madras was new. He wanted to see the whole of it without omitting any place of interest. First, he went to the university from where he should obtain his MA application form. The main door was locked. He glanced around. The University's civic location, its structural art, and the charm of grace were a visual feast.

Soon, the door was opened by the cap man with the colonial bunch of keys still with no sign of rust. Sharp at ten, Hamilton took his application form and left the spot. Out on the lawn was a tree not watered since planted. Under that sat Hamilton with that light blue paper and went through it. When he finished, he felt sure he had understood all it had to say.

Hamilton got up and walked back pondering over the western punch in the application's tone. What was for now clear was he had to urgently load into the application, and its related forms the required personal data. But if you want to say something about yourself, you can't say that. Nobody will believe you. Your declaration about yourself will be taken prima facie as a lie.

To say that you are you, there is a man—a government man. He should say. If he doesn't, you are not you. You are someone else. To make him say that you are you and not any other person is not easy. It is expensive. You should thrust into him a side wage, sometimes in high denominational currency. The moment it is thrust, you become whatever you wish to be. Whatever.

There are some people who wouldn't take the side thrust. They wouldn't sign either. They would drive you to think that their honesty is more inhuman than the smartly operating side wage dharma. The man in charge of Hamilton's area was notorious for his honesty. After his principled honesty is satisfied by his sadistic delay, he would clear your case. Once cleared, the next minute you are reborn as Hamilton the indisputable.

Hamilton was reborn.

The particulars filled and duly signed, Hamilton submitted the application to the university. After that, days dragged on in anticipation of its reply. In the event of a letter coming at this stage, it ought to be the one from the university cap man. He only has business with Hamilton through the Department of Post and Telegram.

After a few days, when a morning dawned, the heavens rained. It was a deafening downpour. From out of the clatter bleated the name of Hamilton twice as from a ram's throat. It was that bleat Hamilton had been waiting for. He went running to the doorstep where the postman was crouching under an umbrella with a hand holding out a mail. Hamilton pulled it out, acknowledged the receipt, unwrapped the cover, and peered. It was 'Madras Christian College'.

Happy as a lark, he folded the paper and stuffed it into his pocket. Not knowing what to do next, he stood at the same spot like a statue, while a series of assails were being launched by doubts. 'What sort of men will the professors of MCC be? Will they be sincere? How will their coaching be? Will it be useful? Will I have to attend all classes, or cut a few and go to Kamala Three Ring Circus? When a professor has left the class, having bored enough, can I steal a few refreshing winks of sleep? How long will I have to read daily? Five hours? Seven hours? Ten hours? Finally, will I pass?' These are academic doubts.

Environmentally, 'This is a western type institution. Will it not be culturally bumpy? Will the porcelain-skinned girls, some of them dazzling like the fashion models, be a distraction? The whole premise is a jungle. Will the jungle be not dark at night? What to do if, in the dark hours, when passing through the jungle alone, a panther that has escaped from Vandalur forest suddenly jumps down from a tree, raises its paw, and bares its teeth to take you in?'

These questions took Hamilton sometime for his senses to come to their right place and react, 'No. Hamilton is different. That difference, this college, whether Christian or Islamic, Buddhist or Jain, Zoroastrian or Shinto cannot destroy. Whatever be the professors, sincere or insincere, their teaching good or bad, Hamilton knows how to pass. If the fashion models give you a full look, you return just a half. Then they will stop giving you any. While walking alone in the jungle, if that forest department panther springs upon you, stunned, why should you go blank? Like Bruce Lee, bring all your energy to the fist of your right hand, and bang its head with all your strength. Turning about a circle and letting out a hiss, the panther will sink to the ground dead. The day it dies, for you, is the day of days. From that day on, you'll be the valiant Samson, the mighty lion killer of MCC.'

For him, these words sounded as from another Hamilton—a stronger fellow inside himself. These words put all his doubts and dreads to flight. In quarter of a minute, Hamilton felt stately like a male president of India, driving on the national highway. All the traffics sidelined by the police to make way for his red-lighted armoured luxury Mercedes Benz.

Part Three

Chapter 55

Admission

Today is his admission. But there was nothing new about the morning he had started for taking it except for that resolution, 'No talk to anyone, known or unknown. Certificates in that new folder, straight to Mambalam Station, ticket, in the train, pocket careful, to the office of the bursar, exchange your pocket for a two-year lease of the college, get back home, and keep mum.'

When that resolution had been carried out, it was evening.

After a hot dinner served by grandma, Hamilton lay on the cot the whole night awake, ruminating, 'Why is it called Madras Christian College? It is not at Madras. It is in another district. Why to locate it a jungle chosen? And after locating, the jungle not removed? How can there be such a big jungle without a monkey? Will that college sundial show the correct time really?'

Chapter 56

Panagal Park-1

It is the next day morning. There was a plan already to go somewhere for a relaxed piece of solitude. Hamilton went down a lane over to Usman Road, jumped into Panagal Park, which offered nothing his eyes would love. Not even a petal of hibiscus. Sat on the cement bench, all with the geographical designs, the Madras crows had sketched.

When he turned his head a few feet at right, as if to welcome him was a brown dog on a high alert. It was brimming with life, tail wagging effusively, but appeared to be in a serious state of indecision. Within seconds, it seemed, it had made up its mind and edged close to him. Lay down quietly ten inches from him, its eyes pointed into his. Hamilton didn't like to be seen so much. He wanted to see it more. When he stared, its face looked like laughing. How good are the dogs of Madras! How smart and gentle! How wise and loving!

Hardly five minutes had passed when it rose to its feet, sniffed the air, and took leave stealthily. Hamilton felt a vacuum. Why the dog came, and after showing him so much love and intimacy, why it exited? The purpose of its visit was a mystery.

Alone at the park, amid the dry leaves, wind fanning what reeked of urine, Hamilton mused, 'There are colleges in India, but the best are the ones that the government runs. There, you can do anything you wish. Sit with the boys in the class and study, stand upon a tree alone and whistle, meow like a cat when the teacher turns to the blackboard, lead a strike and march, and tear the sky shouting, 'Down. Down. Down. The principal down.' These things you can't do in private colleges. They are strict.'

Chapter 57

The Digital Sapiens

In the world, there are two classes of wonders. One is nature-made; another is man-made. Among the man-made wonders, the latest is computer.

What is computer? In a nutshell, a genius, a self-willed genius with an infinite information and use. Understanding, analytical, and sober, except when, under virus, it behaves in accordance with how we treat it.

When man wanted computer as his tool, it was his helper. When he liked it, it was his friend. When he depended on it, it was a partner. When he obeyed it, it was his boss. And he, its office boy.

Computer does both, good and bad. It engages the brain and stupefies the other parts. The stupefied parts unlearn their roles. This unlearning causes a perversion. This perversion is transmitted to the generations to come. Now, man's younger kind has started exhibiting qualities out of line with the normal. It reflects those of computer.

We have become so much one with the computer that our kids in us are losing their identities. In us, they are undergoing disfigurations, physical and mental. The computer generation has become hazy in thought, impaired in vision, slow in feeling.

The present life is one of computer and man combined. The spiritless system and the spirited man are in love. They live lost in mutual adoration. We should not disjoin them. If we do, they can't bear the parting. Unable to bear, they would die, the spirited man first.

All the human resources have been emptied and dumped into computer. Rather surrendered to it. They are its property now. Computer reigns, our decisions are its dictation; and actions, its direction. We have been dragged out of ourselves and modified into the computer-redesigned beings. With our natural senses so much manipulated, we have become ourselves what we call a bio-computer.

The latest advance made by the computer science is into man's private life. At the moment, the silicon and rubber-made animatronically operated life-size human images, assembled as he-man and she-woman are on sale. They are for emergency partners to share life with. When, at a stage, the silicon and rubber partner gives a more exciting partnership, that partnership will become regular. When that becomes regular, the real man and the real woman will split. The real man will live with an unreal woman, and the unreal man will live with a real woman.

Computer is no more a neuter gender. It is masculine, it is feminine, it is a man to a woman and a woman to a man. Intellectually, it is man's better half, and emotionally, his life partner. Jointly, they are trying to breed a new race, a new hybrid race, which Hamilton would name 'Digital Sapiens'.

Chapter 58

Internet

Living beings always love a state of pleasure. To reach it, human beings have many a way. The main way is fun. What is fun? Fun is bringing the laughing side out without burying the grieving side in.

In the past, families arranged fun indoors after dinner. They set up their young ones to provide it; first, male, next female, then both together. The elders directed, kids acted, the neighbours poured in to watch, the fun grew, and also the audience. The space in the house was inadequate, and the site was shifted to a broader spot out in a street. As the fun was played in the street, it was called street play. There, adults joined acting. The audience wanted full view of the players. A stage was erected. The performance given on that was called stage play. The high society people wanted more comfort. Then came roofed sheds with seats into being. Many didn't like the name of stage play, so it was called drama.

In drama, Shakespeare was the king; to begin with, the king of England. His kingdom, having expanded, he is the king of the world. With so much of territory under him, he was not someone who would say that in his dramatic empire, the moon shines green. Level-headed, Shakespeare never spoke an ungainly thing bluntly. If he had to, being a man of literary flourish and creative balance, he did it artfully through his characters, meaning no affront. His humour was not void of vulgarity, but was never in bad taste. As a playwright and a poet, Shakespeare is a magnet. Attracted by it, the people all over the world see his dramas and read his poems, and like England, a lot for his sake. After all, countries are liked for their men of thought, learning, and art.

For the lovers of art, before a thing of beauty, everything else is a zero, be it anything, including an empire. A political empire is but a mushroom. After a day, it darkens, withers, falls in pieces, and is blown away by the wind. But art lives all times afresh and new.

Shakespeare's pen is a wonder. It is a hundred times mightier than the British gun. And his works are a wonder. They are a thousand times more enduring than their empire.

Given a choice between the British throne and Shakespeare's works, Hamilton would seize hold of the latter and get into his cottage gladly to read.

Four score and five years ago, there was an American. A genius. He made it possible for Shakespeare's dramas to be seen in shadows called cinema.

Now, we don't go to theaters. Round the clock shadow entertainer named television is in the drawing room. That shadow entertainer can entertain all the members in the family, but the adults not fully. To meet the full adult requirement, an additional television is positioned in the bedroom, the home's best location for private viewing.

For catering to the sophisticated needs in a special way, has come an invention called Internet. It is not only the world's largest encyclopedia also an inexhaustible time pass, open and forbidden, implicit and explicit. This facility can be owned at home or availed at a shop. All it has to show can't be shared, some are intended to be viewed in singles. To safeguard from being side viewed, the sites open only to the subscribers.

It doesn't end there. There is Internet on the mobile phone too, but its screen is small. To broaden it, shortly a one square inch screen stretchable to12x9 inch width will be connected to it. That will fetch the full effect of the websites to the viewers. It will get popular. The time is not far for the mobile phone without an Internet connection to be regarded as primitive. To Internet, which is a demonic intoxication, most mobile phone users will get addicted. Once addicted, after that, they can't leave it off. In five years' period, the Internet will enslave all the youngsters. To see their children Google ruined, the parents will go distraught.

The next breakthrough the scientists are going to present us will be more ruinous. We don't have to carry anything except, in our memory, a password. Dial it on the mobile phone. The sky becomes a screen, a portion of the sky, that portion of the sky acts as a home theater. On the screen of that home theater spreads out the Garden of Eden. And in that garden, wherever you look, it will be a scene of the progeny of Adam and Eve fast rehearsing their first mistake.

Chapter 59

The Star World

The movie world is not an easy world. It is tough, and fraught with competition. All those who enter that cannot become leading stars. Only a few can. Only they can hold on till their end if they are males, not if females. The female stars despite their face glowing like the moon, on loss of youth, will have to disappear once and for all or reappear as grannies.

Ladies can't defy age. Old age for them may start at any time. The buffer that the powder gives is of an hour, and cream gives is of a day. Not of months or years. For old age, there is no real remedy for women even though cosmetics promise all sorts of miracles. Women's screen position, therefore, is always shaky. At any time, a new face can replace a Venus.

Chapter 60

The Shadows

The entertainment industry is one of immeasurable potential. You can become anybody or anything on the screen, depending a great deal on what you make of your figure. The movie world is the same as the real one, barring just one difference. In the movies, all are shadows. Though shadows, they don't disappoint us because our business ends with seeing. Though ends with seeing, it doesn't end there fully. The shadows teach.

The film theatre is the best of academies. Lessons are taught in air-conditioned halls. Adopting the necessary demonstrative lead, the hero handles classes.

In the first semester, he starts from how to speak a dialogue and passes on to how to sing a song, how to dance, how to smoke, how to booze, how to cheat, how to steal, how to rob, how to burgle, and when caught, how to blabber.

In the second semester, he takes up how to be roguish and how to be obscene; how to join a criminal gang and how to blackmail; how to love a girl, and with her, how to run off; how to marry her, and the next day, how to divorce.

In the third semester, he handles how to fight with hands, how to fight with sword, how to fight with rifle, how to fight with grenade, how to shoot down a copter, how to hijack a plane, how to hold the passengers hostage, how to negotiate terms, how to set a deadline for ransom, and if the ransom move doesn't work, how to gun down the crew and passengers, and how to blow up the plane, how to get nabbed, how to be charge sheeted, how to face a trial, how to get convicted, how to take a capital sentence, and how to get thrown into a prison.

There is another semester also which is the last. That is an advanced study. It is on how to move the appellate jury; if it doesn't help, how to approach the constitutional head, how to wait for his mercy, and finally, how to be let off or get hanged.

Chapter 61

Panagal Park-2

Hamilton was still on the bench at the Panagal Park, not conscious of the traffic noise and the vendors' strain. When feeling drowsy, down at his pant, he felt a tug. It was the dog again, his Madras animal visitor, Brown. They stayed fixed into the eyes of each other for a short while, then they dropped their heads. Not ten minutes had passed, Brown was in a mood for leaving. Its leaving mood brought into Hamilton a law, which you may call the law of Brown. The law is, 'No living being goes to another living being except for taking something from.'

Look at the living beings including the Madras human beings. All go, some on foot, some on wheels, and some on flight. But in all cases, the speed of their going is monitored by the urge for taking. Taking something from somebody who may be:

1) Obliged to give
2) Half obliged to give
3) Ever ready to give
4) Half ready to give
5) Not at all ready to give

6) Does not have to give
7) Should not give
8) Should not give at all
9) Should not give even at the cost of his or her life

To take what from Hamilton, Brown has come? To take something he has scented somehow. That, Hamilton is ready to give. The chocolates in his pocket. He took out two pieces and placed them on the bench. Brown sprang to its feet and bounced thrice. Then, he picked one. The other, he ignored and went away pleased. Hamilton's eyes followed Brown, which, when going the chocolate in mouth, was shouted into a run by the city loafers who had come there numbering about ten.

What type of loafers are they? And what type of takers? Who would be their target? Hamilton had in his pocket fifteen rupees for fueling his uncle's Standard Super Ten. For the sake of its safety, he changed over to another bench in the park's northeastern corner. On the pavement were two policemen tasting tea sip by sip, between sips, exchanging sneeze.

Tea finished, the policemen left. Hamilton sensed danger. He didn't like to stay there. Who will stay in the same place longer than it is safe? He looked in the direction Brown had gone. No Brown there or anywhere. Hamilton took a sitting doze, got up, dusted his back, lobbed into his mouth a chocolate, and walked home slowly chewing it all the way.

Chapter 62

Elizabeth and Cleopatra

A lady came to England, the daughter of the ruler of that country as its queen. She was young, full of her mother's charm and father's stubbornness, Mother's tenderness of face, and Father's robustness of heart.

She is the opposite of another woman, an Egyptian lady of Greek origin—Cleopatra. She was first the wife of her one brother then the wife of her another brother, then the wife of Julius Caesar, and finally, the girlfriend of Mark Antony.

The tempestuous Cleopatra married marriage after marriage. The temperate English queen threw to the wind offer after offer. No lady born to a human couple compared with Cleopatra in the female spell. The Bard of Avon, struck to gaze at her from Antony's angle, went off with his verse that speaks volumes of her 'infinite variety'. To enjoy the beauty and power of imagination in that rousing verse to a fair measure, there should be a subtle amalgamation of 'young in age and old in knowledge'. Her love and beauty are an eternal talk, but they did her no good. Only caused her fall and ruined her kingdom.

What a great lesson it is for the queen of England, learnt from Cleopatra, the whirlwind of romance! Would she love and love a man? Would she marry and marry him really? She had understood that an unmarried woman is time-proof. Age can exercise no sway on her. It can't bend her shape or sap he face, shrink her skin or dull her shine.

Her unmarried maidenhood coupled with love resistant singleness inspired the men of England. They turned them into authors, poets, singers, administrators, diplomats, soldiers, sailors, manufacturers, storekeepers, and salesmen. She wove the dreams of overseas trade and worldwide commerce.

Her court was decorated with select lords and select peers. Ladies were kept out prudently. Her country was set to one tone—tone of national honour. This unprecedented sense of honour and unity achieved initially by her, raised England higher and higher, and eventually into an empire. Shrewd and canny, she learnt all that were regally required from the falls and flops of the past rulers.

Her charm prevailed on many, poetically on Edmund Spenser. That Faerie Queen is Queen Elizabeth I, the daughter of King Henry VIII.

Now, from the quirky corner of Hamilton's head, rises a question, 'If a woman could make in the world a history of such an unexcelled glory, why its formula should not be exploited for the greater good of our race as a whole?' At the moment, we need a woman at whose beauty the entire menfolk should fall into an irredeemable enchantment. Is there one such on this earth? Certainly No. No after Helen of Troy.

Fellows speak about cloning. At the same time, a section of orthodoxy is opposed to the new people coming to us other than through the natural track. If that opposition is revoked, and a stunner Helen cloned, then many of our woes could be brought to an end, especially those caused by the terrorists. If the news of the beauty of that cloned Helen reaches them, the terrorists kicking their AK47 away will go down on their knees begging for the look of her visage. One Helen cloned for the world to start with, and then one each for a country.

Chapter 63

The Electric Train -I

About the airways, there are so many things that we should know. But at that time for knowing, for Hamilton, there were only three:

1) The inventor/s of the plane
2) The airport names of Delhi, Calcutta, and Bombay
3) The first woman pilot

This is enough for a good student. The other things like the owner of the air service, cost of the craft, make of the craft, the craft's capacity, the power of the engine, the jet blade RPM. Take off speed, flying speed, flying height, landing angle. Aviator's qualification, the number of the cabin crew, the age, education, height, weight, and the colour of the air hostess were not necessary.

The French man made, the British man gave, and here the Madras man flies, but all the Madras men can't fly. They should be air fit. What is air fit? It is extra money. It may be any money. Father's money, Father-in-law's money, government money, company money, money looted in politics, cheated in business, robbed in banks, waylaid on highways, stolen in houses, minted in drugs, pocketed in gambling, or netted in whoring. These are the ones who mainly make the payload.

What do the others do? Others watch. Watch the plane in the sky wide-eyed. They don't take what blasts their eardrums as an air quake. For them, it is the extra money generated space symphony.

The prime minister and the president fly special carriers. The prime minister flies on business. The president on good will visits.

We know every year comes a monsoon that floods the nation and drowns the cities. Madras floats. To see how it floats, flies a helicopter. From that, a minister looks down to the great joy of the people who have lost their huts to the flood. The flying shot of the minister when repeatedly telecast, the rain soaked hungry children forget their hunger, seeing him on the government TV.

The men of the west longed to be men of the world—the whole world. But the men of Madras show no interest to become the men of even their own city. For a Madras man to be one of the full city, he must first come out of his house. Do a bit of roaming in the metro electric train.

Men and women, boys and girls, whom their families have pushed out to win the bread of the day, of the week, of the month, or of the life after years of carrying the back-breaking loads of books account for the train's passenger weight.

The electric train is never a monotony. How many engaging features inside! The air that cools from the ever running black fans, the business ads on the walls, the full-throated calls of the map venders, the dance and music of the train beggars, drunken men swearing in the foulest of obscene words, women in the venders' coach locked in blouse ripping fights, and the anonymous porn drawings left halfway.

While passing the track close to Meenambakkam before Tirusulam came, the electric train used to run excitedly. At the drumbeat of the wheels and the rocking of the compartments, lulled into a slumber, the heads of the seated passengers would rotate. And some of the heads would sag in front over and over again until about to bodily roll down.

At that time, if a plane lands or takes off, shaken from the slumber by its whirring noise, they would turn their heads the airport way. But before they would catch the glimpse of anything in full, either the plane is gone or the train is in the next station.

Chapter 64

Fancy for Lamborghini

In using the sky, our kings were great. They had not only palanquins, elephant litters, and horse chariots, also aeroplanes. But those kings are not kings anymore. With their kingship, their planes are also gone. Next to them, certain royal ladies and movie women, it is said, had their own four-seaters.

It is not known why, in India, so many of the clever men and clever women are done with the land vehicles. What happened to the list of the richest, and those at the bursting point in Swiss lockers?

Some gift planes, but when they gift, they gift only to one in the family, not more. Why not more? The future readers would have told that it is unsafe for a family to own more than two planes. If they own, it would negatively influence their zodiac power resulting in the loss of their income tax cases.

Rich people know how difficult it is to be rich, and at the same time, truthful to the income tax law. They want to be truthful, and at the same time, don't want to earn to pay it all for tax, so they go by the word of their future predictors.

If the tax law is made flexible, some of those who could take fancy for Lamborghini Aventador LP 700-4 could be found in the sky droning in copters, bringing more of the celestial space under human use. It would be good if the human use increases. If restricted, the space will be jammed with rockets, the rockets of America, China, Iran, and India.

The Indian sky scientists have gotten smart now. Their space technology has picked up. It has become incredibly vertical. Now when sent up, the Sriharikota rockets don't take U-turns.

Chapter 65

The Electric Train- 2

Where a human being is, there will all his activities be. Picking the pocket is out and out human. Other species don't practise it. It happens often in the electric trains. The first time travelers are particularly vulnerable. If a purse is picked, a loud squeal is let off. Then you can see the alertness of the passengers and a double alertness of whose money already lost to a cutpurse.

The seasoned women travel in the ladies' compartment. The fresh ones in common bogies accompanied by males for help.

The rush hour travel in the Madras suburban railways is quite a sight. It is nothing short of a live demonstration of fitness for survival. The qualities like strength and adventurousness, daring and foolhardiness essential for modern life, could be seen working to a perilous degree. The young men hang sticking out in hundreds like the honeybees on the sides of the train that leaves the station raising a hell of a hoot. That travel you must enjoy. A great thrill. Want a greater thrill? Go to Delhi. For the greatest, we have Bombay.

Usually, the railway employees, and those with no taste for memorable train experiences prefer the first class. Hamilton feels that this first class can be spared for the free use of those who live on the post-service grace pay. If spared, it will be something like a recompense for the indignity they suffer from the subject clerks dealing with their pension papers and medical claims.

Chapter 66

The Beggars

Today, we can reach Delhi from London in eight hours and twenty minutes by air. In old times, it was wearisome. The sea voyage from England to India via Cape of Good Hope took from nine months to one year.

To come to India, what a lot of trouble the British men have taken seafaring thousands of miles on the high waves, some being thrown overboard by storm, some slipping into water, some vomiting for sea odour, some falling ill for tropical heat, some going mad at the unresting expanse of the tidal surges. Despite all these, they came. What for? Not for helping Indians. Then for what? To make a name? Name as what? Name as a power. A world power. World power number one.

Did they make that name? Yes, they did. Is it with them? No, not now. What happened? The name so made didn't last. They didn't know that they would lose and lose it so soon. When winning the countries, they were growing great. When returning them to their owners, they dropped in greatness—quite like the earlier imperialists history has listed out.

It seems for imperialism, also there is a specific pattern for beginning, growing, and ending. Now, the present thinkers view that imperialism is a madman's passion, an urge, an urge to expand his territory. Expand for what? Expand only to shrink. Shrink to its original size, sometimes to shrink to smaller than the original, sometimes much smaller, sometimes regrettably smaller.

Some observers who are sharp prick that the imperialists should have first looked after their kitchen garden properly before trying to bring other nations under their plough.

If you widen your territory, your administration should be effective uniformly. For that, you will have to be economically self-generative and self-sustained. Else, it is not sagacious to think oneself big. If you think yourself big, there is a problem. You come under a necessity—necessity to show it off. To show it off in the ruling sense of a nation, there is only one way. You should maintain an army as would synchronize with the bigness claimed. Most countries that are large are obsessed with that army kind of greatness.

Small countries are small including in the revenue they earn. Their budget is so, as their revenue. Within that small budget, they can't accommodate a nuclear ambition. Monaco doesn't make bombs; Nauru, rockets; Tuvalu, satellites. We know their land width and population strength. They are a challenge that the big nations must learn their political, social, and economic lessons from the small ones. Does Vatican have an army? Is it nuclear? Does it test explosions? What is the largest thing it has? The library.

Vatican is small even for a village. It is in the size of a hostel. In that small place, people are known to one another like in Heber Hall. They can't hide their names, addresses, and activities. In a country of Vatican size, the government is real. Because it is real, its people are all rich. Are there beggars in Vatican?

There are beggars in the world, but most are where the countries are large. If a country is too large, the beggars will be too many in number, and too beggarly in beggarliness. The beggars' call, you can hear from where you live, where you work, where you rest, where you shop, where you travel, and where you go to greet a God.

We have plans and schemes, but all have failed to get the beggars off begging. In solving the problem of beggars, we are not more successful than in solving the problem of mosquitoes. However, to actually solve, Hamilton's suggestion is give the beggars each a ration card, then he is a social being. Enter his name in the voters' list, then he is a political being. Let him vote, he learns politics. Once he has learnt politics, to get rich, he will take not long. Within five years, he will be exporting granite to Japan.

Chapter 67

Some Hang, Some Behead

The inventions that revolutionise our life are the works of some rare men. But those who benefit from the inventions do not honour the inventors. The few who honour do not honour appropriately. The honouring styles differ. They differ from country to country. Some countries worship them, some insult them, some praise them, some exile them, some put behind bar, some neck into cell, some hang, some behead, some set on fire.

We should but appreciate the British. For the inventors, they erect statues and dedicate them to their memory. The Indian inventions are many, and the most widely known, zero. Because it is zero, it should not be thought small. Zero is one of the greatest inventions. For any number to end honourably, it should end with the Indian invention. Though there is nothing in zero, in no other number, there is so much beauty and so much fullness. The more the concluding zeros, the greater the status of that number. All people love zero, and they love it to end as the last digits.

Zero has a power. It brings people close to India. Any man who can count up to ten is numerically one-tenth an Indian. His numerical closeness to India is as much as he uses zero. Through a single cheque drawn for a million dollars from a bank, an American becomes six times an Indian.

If the contemporary ruler had the fore-knowledge that the invention of his mathematician would go to China, Europe, Middle East, and to the whole world, and make him so great, you know what he would have done? He would have killed him by thrusting molten lead into his throat. Luckily for this mathematical genius of Rajasthan, it didn't happen. Maybe his king was either of a guilt-free conscience or exceptionally magnanimous.

Chapter 68

Sighed a Bucket

In Madras Christian College, the first day of Hamilton's class began with an introduction. Ladies said a low-key hello with a glint of gentle smile, while the males shook hands till they got twisted into a crowbar.

Introduction over, they waited in the class for work to begin. One teacher came, took attendance, lectured, and went his way the left side. Another teacher came, did the same thing, and went his way the right side. Thus, passed the forenoon, left and right.

After lunch came the professor parking under a tree his cycle as old as MacMillen's first piece. A white clad fair man, no older than fifty, head radiant, face insistent, sleeves folded, shoes black, no socks. High-waist baggy trousers buckled in a white belt, entered the class, took his position, saw the face of no boy, saw the face of no girl. Boys seated five feet in front. Girls, seven feet right. Spoke no word to any. There was nothing warm, nothing social, and nothing personal.

His lecture that commenced most dutifully went on a rhythmic pace. But long before it ran out, the bell rang a peal. He collected his work tools, simultaneously collected himself, and hurried back to his dear cycle waiting for him under the same tree.

All was not well, everything frightful. Some of the students felt like having entered a wrong place to study, and Hamilton sighed a bucket.

Chapter 69

Search

Men and women studied in this college, but men were more. The management, however, didn't care to correct the imbalance. If women were as many, it would have been better. More women means more resolve, more study, better results, and greater name to the college.

Most women were Christians. In church services, the female presence was twice the male. A 55-year-old lady from USA, a student of MA (Philosophy), was a regular service participant apart from the French professor couple. The diamond boys were all Christians. The Mongolian youngsters never turned up the church side. One of Hamilton's classmates, a Tinnaveli godly soul, taught the Sunday Classes.

We all know Christ. Christ was born in a cow shed to a virgin mom as a male baby. He was raised as a carpenter boy, heard as a preacher, witnessed as a miracle worker, betrayed as a blasphemer, hanged as a criminal, interred as dead. On the third day, seen as resurrected, lived as the second timer, watched as ascended, said as preparing places of joy in heaven, and believed as he will come down again and take there all who followed him truly. So much Christianity Hamilton learnt not as a student. Only later.

This college, which has been teaching thousands and thousands of students, is Christian. It has produced more than a hundred eminent people, both men and women. However, the four of every five of them are not Christians. Why? Search.

Chapter 70

The Merchant and the King

Long ago, an English diplomat visited India. He met the emperor at his court. A seat was offered, he didn't take, and he stood bowing low in awe of the ruler. His sitting was insisted. That royal insistence was overcome by his show of deference. There were more of nods and less of words with the Englishman. The persistent show of the western courtesy moved his majesty greatly. Pleased with the waxed moustache, trimmed beard, and the perfect sideburns of the fine looking Englishman in his humble carriage, the Indian monarch granted certain villages to start his trade.

We know events work always to a plan. In the east-west deal, they worked as though clearly predetermined.

Days passed. The Englishman slowly moved up from his village to Firka. The emperor, hookah in mouth, came gradually down from empire to kingdom. Months passed. The Englishman moved from his Firka to Taluk. The king slid down from his kingdom to princedom. Years passed. From Taluk, the Englishman crawled up to district. The prince came down from princedom to pettydom. Decades passed. The petty ruler came down to Firka and the Englishman pushed up to statedom. A century passed. Then the Firka man dropped to the village and the Englishman rose to the empire.

It was a triumphant scene of the west going uphill, and a dismal scene of the east coming downhill. When the Englishman bowed his bow, he saw in mind his empire. When the emperor believed the gesture, he didn't see his village.

It is here there is a lesson for the college teachers to learn and to follow it in letter and spirit. Like the Indian emperor, they must come down and down to the students and teach. Then only the students like the British will go up and up in their studies and rise in future to their empire; otherwise, the hopes of rise would fall and they would go back to their village to cultivate cotton with coriander as inter-crop.

Chapter 71

The Syllabus

Hamilton wanted to study his MA syllabus. When he went through, he found that the detailed texts were dozens; non-detailed books two hundred, criticism three hundred, supplementary reading the rest of the books in the library. Not one library, so many. One at the university, one at Presidency, two at Madras Christian, one at the British council, and one more at the Connemara.

Chapter 72

Pocket-Sized Handy Remake

Whenever Hamilton thought of his syllabus, it gave him a shudder followed by an irritation. After a close scrutiny, the conclusion he reached was, 'This syllabus is like the Pacific Ocean. In it, the student may swim and swim, but would never reach the other shore. To reach the other shore, the syllabus should be within his swimming strength. For that, the syllabus should not be the university original. It should be his own. A pass easy, pocket-sized handy remake. 'How to remake?' This question ran a hundred metre race inside his head. And at length, he found an answer, which was simple. Like preparing a chicken sixty-five.

To start with, smash the university syllabus, cut off its head and its legs, skin the hide, remove the entrails, take out the bones. Now, it is soft, cut, slice, wash, and spice properly. Now, the syllabus is ready for the next stage of processing.

Take it to the stove, fry it in oil. Fry in correct heat and to the correct point. Though it takes some doing, it is here Hamilton's syllabus is cooked. His concise personalised version, not anymore an ocean, just a tub. Now, the syllabus and exam have been joined, the exam and hope have been bridged, and Hamilton and pass are a made for each other duo.

For doing a work well, Hamilton never seeks the blessings of the holy men. For Hamilton, he is his own high priest. Saintly, except in some small respects with the help of his self-made syllabus, as duck to water, he took to his round the clock invocation for a pass.

This syllabus, remaking none, would do for you. Not the university, not the college, not the professor, only yourself. Hamilton knows very well that he is a fool, fool of the worst order, yet he trusted his foolishness. Ultimately, it is that foolishness, which helped him more than the wisdoms of the Solomons of MCC and the Acharyas of Presidency.

Chapter 73

The Victim of the Potter

Hamilton, in the long run, realised one thing beyond any doubt. The student days are not the right time to enjoy literature. Literature can be well enjoyed after the exam, better enjoyed after post-graduation, and best enjoyed after quitting office.

The student days are there to be used for a pass, only a pass—a good pass. Some in their student days turned over the pages of the notes borrowed from the girls of Stella Mary's in addition to the volumes bought at the bookshop and lent by all the libraries known. But The Indian Express showed them no mercy.

These fallouts make a class of syllabus victims, a disconsolate class unable ever to get over the malaise. They need to be helped, but how? For that, a fact finding cell should be formed in each college. It must go into the causes of those fatalities. The findings will facilitate, to a large extent, to tune up the teacher with his job.

The teacher is a teacher not just for the class, but also the teacher for the students individually. This, the teacher should remember. He shouldn't stop with sowing knowledge, also should watch over. If the knowledge doesn't germinate, he should look out for the canker, remove it, and water. This should be there at all levels. More at post-graduation. Failing at post-graduation is not the same as failing at kindergarten. The damage here is hard to repair.

A bright boy needs no teacher. A good teacher is needed where the boys are slow. The entire teaching should be focused on the slowest. Then no boy in the class will fail.

It is after all the professor who selects his students. Then why should he select a student whom he can't make pass? Once a student fails, what should be done to the professor? Give him not a hanging. Hanging is too severe a punishment. Give him half the pay till his failed boy has passed.

The jungle is green as ever, the buildings stand as ever, teachers teach, and students learn as ever. The business goes on as ever. But what about him who has failed? He has become an orphan of his alma mater, a forgotten creature, a postgraduate abortion after two years of sleepless conceiving. After abortion, none to think of. None to care for. A discarded boy, he becomes a frustrated self-hater, a victim of the potter who chose him for his clay.

Hamilton felt wrecked to meet three of such sad cases later—two boys and one girl. For some least expected causes, if someone has flunked, how to help him out? The professor should arrange tuition. Not a paid tuition, but a free tuition, and see that he has got through the next time.

Is there one such selfless good soul in the teaching community? If there were any, Hamilton would meet early and give that person a warm hug. But Hamilton, in his days, heard of no such man or woman in the city and the state of Madras.

Chapter 74

The Game of Boxing

To pass requires a clear idea of what exam and valuation are. If the students have an overriding view, it is an offence to the examiner; and if they write it, a disrespect. Examiners don't want anything that they don't know or don't want to agree with. In literature, they want sentences idiomatically correct and sensibly obedient. Bold statements will be uncivil and grammar mistakes, fatal. The only error not considered seriously for failing a student relates to the punctuation rules. That may be for the cause the uses of certain punctuation marks are an unending wrangle.

What is exam? It is a game of boxing you play with the examiner on the answer sheet. For playing it well in literature, at the first hit, you should knock the examiner down and form a cramp. After that, the hits you deliver should be cramp-relieving massages that he should welcome. All the cramp-relieving hits should not be perfect hits. There should be a few mishits too here and there. Then your examiner would like you and your paper more.

What is valuation? It is an affair between the paper that you write and the head that reads. It is taken up mostly as a post-dinner domestic night duty. While valuing, if the mood of the examiner turns sideways, it is a sign that the time is bad for you. In mathematics, the sideway turning and mood digression don't affect the student destiny much. The last few symbols are mainly seen. If correct, 100 per cent.

Literature is not so. Its answer is a blend of right and wrong. Every answer. The one who values it would tell how much is right. He never tells how much is wrong, it is implied. To get through, one can be wrong up to 65 per cent, not more. It is always bad to ask anyone for a full right answer. For the same answer you write, a dozen evaluators would award a dozen different grades. There is no answer that is fully right, and no answer that is fully wrong in literature. There are only these two: one, lucky answer; another, unlucky answer. Your answer is either this or that depending in large part on the valuation man, the valuation time, and the valuation mood.

Chapter 75

A Thousand in All

Hamilton often wondered when life is real, and not very unsuited to live, why man seeks art, the unreal, and of only a short-lived pleasure. On a closer look, he found that our first love is only for short-lived pleasures.

Man is life, life is energy, energy is motion, not a straight line motion. Life hates it, life hates straightness. It loves a motion of a confused sort. Can it be zigzag? No. Can it be curve? No. Can it be concentric? No. Can it be eccentric? No. There is an order of a kind in all these.

Life doesn't like order in any form, it wants disorder—utter disorder. That disorder shouldn't be for long hours. It should be just for a short minute. If over, it looks for another disorder. Life doesn't want the same disorder the same way twice. It must change. Keep changing. If it doesn't, the man will change, and get disorderly.

No man is in a spot more than a second. He keeps fleeting in imagination. Sitting in the same spot, in one hour, he lives in sixty into sixty spots in mind. These three thousand and six hundred spots provide the changes that his mind wants. If that changing stops, his balance will be disturbed. When balance is disturbed, madness will set in. A normal man is one in whom the second-to-second change is occurring. That is an invisible occurrence. We are both the same and different every second.

It is not the stretch of sameness; it is the ever occurring changes we want, our systems want, our senses want—all the five senses and mind. We don't get enough of them in the real life, but we want them. Any source is all right. So to get them in plenty, we seek extra life situations. Through these situations, we get the changes we need for living without a hitch.

The kings of the past met their need of changes. How? By listening to the lies their court buffoons lied. The queens of the past met their need of changes. How? By laughing over the lies their court clowns lied. We, too, meet our need of changes. How? By reading, watching, and listening to lies. Jungle stories, Internet images, and cell phone lotteries. What are they? Downright lies.

Changes engage man. They keep him happy and harmless too. A new thing is a change. A new friend is a good change. A new woman is a powerful change. Read the history of kings who, in addition to their palace packed with wives, had outside a huge township of concubines. Such kings were good fellows. They didn't like to go out, fight, and kill much. Only those kings who eschewed these harmless pleasures resorted to harm others.

There was, long ago, a king in Israel. Of all the males, the human race produced, it is he who husbanded ladies in four digits. How many exactly? Seven hundred wives and three hundred concubines. A thousand in all—a world record. That king was a fine man. He fought not even ten battles.

His father was also a king. That poor king had less than ten wives. He fought the maximum number of battles. How many? More than a thousand.

Chapter 76

Music

What is music? Music is something to be heard and to be stopped at that, not asked what. The one who defines it may be a master of grammar in music, but never of the kind we would love to hear. Yet, some have told, in their own way, what music is. They vary in words, but mean the same—music is sweet.

Music is one of the art powers that takes us to the height of intense delight, the rises and falls of the singer's voice, the notes and beats and strokes and vibrations of the instruments could render. Among the few who captivate Hamilton through music, the one who captivated him the most is the king of the soft melody, the vocalist-composer-director of South India. His wife paired with him as a playback partner. In the domain of South Indian melody, he reigned supreme during the third quarter of the last century. Now he is no more. His musical journey ended in a train.

In music, the Indian women are unexcelled. They are comfortable with veena, violin, and pound of thigh. Not with guitar or drum. How nice it will be if in India too, women do something independently.

Why here, no all-woman orchestra like in Cuba or Austria or England? Why they don't form one? They won't. Certainly won't. They are difficult beings. Women can't put up with women. They can't get along as a company. In India, an all-woman set up is always self-abortive, but women sing a lot.

Hamilton would say in the whole world, India is unique in the musical gift. We have a flair for the use of voices and instruments. Once these are set under right inspiration, they lift us high and hold in a state of heavenly bliss. Thousand times heard, they won't surfeit. We lose ourselves into the rapturous excitement with the authors for their lyrics, vocalists for their voice, instrumentalists for their back up, and the directors for their genius.

Listen to some of the early numbers of those musical wizards of West Bengal. Also, some of theirs remade in Europe. Compare. We will find the true stature of the Indian music.

Hamilton ranks Bollywood as the world headquarters of melody with sub-headquarters most of which are in India only. India has grown self-sufficient in music, even surplus lately. All countries know that. Hollywood is proposing to import our music.

Export. Export. Not to Hollywood alone. Everywhere export. Indianize music all globe. Then only one day, we can trumpet a proclamation that in the Indian musical empire, the stars shine violet.

Chapter 77

PG House

On a stroll down the memory lane, what excites Hamilton most is his hall with his hallmates. Heber postgraduate house is a beautifully designed student abode. It is comely with a compact structure. The building has a fencing wall. Not difficult to cross by one jump for a late night movie. Certain nights would be a series of jumps performed with least disturbance to the watchman croaking with his snores like a lonely frog at the gate.

In the house is an enclosed space used to play improvised games. On weekends there, that ever laughing physics fellow would bring out the bits of a Chemmeen song from his hand-made radio. That chemistry chap, rash and boyish, would stretch a rainbow from some laboratory liquid. That botany guy, calm and composed, would create a mini-park holding his old guitar in one hand and Charminar Gold in the other. The zoology creatures, embedded in hibernation, would come out to see the light of the day ten minutes before breakfast. The art fellows, finishing an afternoon nap, would step down half steady. After a minute of mixing, they would make a face and log out.

Chapter 78

Hamilton Trapped in Library

That day evening, classes over, Hamilton as usual went to the PG Library to spend an hour on books. The PG Library was at the first floor of the main library. Though designated as PG Library, all students can use it. Books there were voluminous, many of them leather-bound, some covered with mold, and some damaged by book-borers. Most books remain uncared, untouched, unopened, unread. For a change, that evening, Hamilton wanted to take and read the biggest book whatever the subject. He searched and found one, which he lifted in both his hands and set it on a table. The cover that was strong like a metal sheet showed the picture of an old man, milk white hair covering all his head, leaving the top part for a considerable baldness. Hamilton guessed he should be the one who discovered that man has come from monkey, Charles Darwin. The volume was less of letters and more of pictures commencing from amoeba. Since it contained the pictures of the whole of animal kingdom, it was so absorbing. Since it was so absorbing, the passing of time was not felt by

Hamilton. When he looked about, he found that all students had left excepting him and a girl.

The ceiling fan that was running was heating him with hot air. He thought he should rush for a natural air in a roofless place outside, but he could not leave the girl to her fate. He should either tell her and go, or take her and go. What to tell and how to? She was copying something seriously. He went hesitantly, stood by, but spoke to her no word. Sensing his presence that was so close, she dropped the pen, raised her head, saw him sharply, and in a tone of disgust asked, 'What?'

He, like a watchman to his mistress, answered caringly, 'All have gone except you and me. I have to go now. If I am also gone, you will be alone. Now time is 6.10, it will get dark soon.'

She glanced around and said, 'Oh, you are right.'

At once, she rose up, pen and notebook in hand. Then both hurried toward the door. It was closed. Hamilton pulled the knob. Again, with force. And again and again, pulled with more and more of force, it didn't open. Brought the top bolt down. And bottom bolt up. Now, he pulled the knob, door didn't open. Every time he pulled, there was a sound of metallic jam on the other side of the door. The street lights got lit.

Hamilton sweated in fear, and the girl trembled in fright. Tears welled up in her eyes and dropped down like pearls. She's very upset, broke into sobs, mildly at first and within minutes, loudly. She peered through the window at her back. It was already getting dark. She turned this way and that, and noted that the fan was running, books lay scattered, cupboards stood like giants, and the library hall was large. Then she turned her eyes to Hamilton who had gone pale. He was feeling helpless, feet getting cold. Both stood at the same spot thinking things and fearing fears to themselves. Both wanted to speak but knew not what. Though speaking will not help, to hear a voice would be a comfort, a sort of comfort.

Moments rolled in silence when the girl sank down to the floor. Hamilton didn't do as she did. He kept standing. Now, the most important thing is either he or she should speak something. That will make a beginning of something. Hamilton was attempting to open his mouth, but feared the consequences.

Looking fixedly at the fan running over where she was taking notes, the girl gathered boldness and asked in a low voice, 'What to do?

Hamilton, after a long minute of finding what to say, replied with the same question with two words added to it, 'What shall we do?'

Silence persisted like their sworn enemy. How to overcome it to establish a line of fearless communication was their first concern. The girl proved to be resourceful.

She rose up with an air of determination. When she stood, she was to his neck that made him jittery. Yet, he looked at her straight and she at him. They got bridged somewhat. In a feeble whisper, she suggested, 'Shall we both go, stand near the window, and cry for help?'

'Okay, good idea.'

'Come, follow me'

They marched to the window. Before they reached, she changed her mind, 'If we cry, will it not be awkward? If the evening walkers see us together what will they think of us? Better let us not do that.'

He responded, 'Okay, good.'

They retreated to where they were first. She to where she was taking notes, and he to where he was with Charles Darwin. The distance between them about eight feet. On an impulse to know about him, she asked, 'By the way, your name?'

'Hamilton.'

'Christian?'

'Yea, yours?'

'Pinky Pop.'

'Jain?'

'Yea. What does Hamilton mean?'

'I don't know. What does Pinky Pop mean?'

'I also don't know. Why are you that far? Come near. Sit here in a chair.'

Still at heart with quite a lot of fear, Hamilton inched toward her and took that chair.

'What do you do here?'

'MA.'

'Subject?'

'Literature.'

'Bennet Albert?'

'Yes, how do you know?'

'From how you fear.'

'You?'

'I do research.'

'In what?'

'Philosophy.'

'Krishnamachary.'

'Yes, how do you know?'

'From how bold you are.'

'Can you tell me what is philosophy?'

'I don't know actually. It is a subject. Tell, what is literature?'

'I also don't know. It is also a subject.'

'Where do you stay?'

'Heber. You?'

'Women's hostel.'

'Where?'

'Chrompet.'

'Will not anyone search for you?'

'Matron will. You?'

'Warden will. What to tell them if they ask?

'Tell what had happened.'

'Fine.'

She asked, 'Can I call you Ham?'

'Sure. Can I call you Pinky?'

'Sure.'

He said, 'Dinner?'

'No dinner.'

'Water?'

'No water.'

'Milk?'

'No milk, we can take everything double tomorrow, Ham.'

'How to spend this night?'

'Sleep.'

'Where?'

'You on that table. Me on this table.'

'Good idea'

'Do you snore?'

'Sometimes.'

'Not this night, please.'

'I will not.'

They retired to their chosen tables to sleep on, but they didn't lie down.

'Pinky, you know there is no toilet here.'

'No problem. Fortunately, we are in hostels, Ham. If we are at home, our parents will go crazy to miss us the whole night.'

'You are right, Pinky.'

'Ham, do you believe in ghosts?

'I don't.'

'In the nights can you go out to the graveyard?'

'Even at midnight—alone.'

'Then why you sweated so much standing at the door?'

'At that time, I don't know why, I thought of Bennet Albert.'

'You are really good and gentle. I like you.'

'Thanks.'

'You are really bold and independent. I like you too.'

'Thanks.'

'What is time, Ham?'

'Half past eight, thirteen hours more to get out of here, it is our good luck that today is not Friday.'

'What if?'

'We will have to serve this imprisonment for an additional forty-eight hours.'

'I hate that fellow, that dirty fellow for locking us in like this for no fault of ours.'

'For the fault of our being true to our studies.'

'Who would have done this?'

'I am also asking who would have done this.'

'I have an uncle, Ham. He is a police inspector.'

'Where?'

'In Washermenpet Police Station. Immediately, after our release, we will go to our hostels. There, what we should do is first, do a good toilet, take a good bath, change into a clean dress, take a heavy breakfast, four slices of bread, double omelette and double cup of milk, and enough water. I will give you my hostel address. Come there at eleven o'clock. We will go to Washermenpet Police Station.'

'Excellent, Pinky, but will not our principal get angry with us for not informing him first?'

'If he wants to get angry, let him get angry with that rascal. Why with us? Ham, look, it is no good telling our principal. If we tell him first, he will put upon the notice board a warning cautioning the students not to indulge in such mischief. On the notice board, your name and mine will appear. If they don't appear also, our boys will somehow find out. Then it will become a scandal. I am already engaged to my cousin, a company executive in Singapore. If we tell my uncle, he will come in plain clothes, meet the principal, with his permission investigate discreetly, catch that fellow, and book him under some section. Police inspectors know how to handle such guys.'

'Good idea, Pinky, ask your uncle to put him in a room with no light, no window, all dark, no food, no water, no toilet, all stench. He should put him in with a worst baboon for company. Let him suffer like that one month.'

'One month?'

'Yes, thirty days.'

'He will die.'

'Let him die. He deserves it. Are we not dying now? When Joseph, such an innocent man, has suffered so much in a cell, why not he?'

'Who is that Joseph?'

'That is a big story. I will tell later.'

'Let the fan run. Let us not switch on light. It will be too bright to sleep.'

'Pinky, do you think we can really sleep? Are not mosquitoes biting you? Noah made a mistake. He should have left out mosquitoes when he loaded the specimens in his arc.'

'Who is Noah?'

'That is another story I will tell later. When pushing that fellow into the dark room, please ask your uncle to fill it with as many mosquitoes as he can. Let that fellow understand what mosquito bite is.'

Both lay down, but didn't sleep. There was silence. Ham heard the sound of a slap. 'What is that, Pinky?'

'You are right, Ham. There are mosquitoes here.'

Then after sometime, Pinky heard Ham slapping himself. Then Ham, Pinky, then each heard the other slapping at regular intervals. Then both heard both of them slapping. Ham violently. After a while, the slapping stopped.

Time had been passing. The world had been sleeping. They didn't know all that. They had also been sleeping their own share of sleep on the hard wood with no bed spread, no pillow, and no blanket. Birds declared the dawn and got noisy at which Pinky got up with a start.

'Ham, what is the time?'

Ham answered readily, 'Five thirty. In one hour, it will be bright. In four hours, we will be out.'

They were scratching wherever the mosquitoes had bitten. Pinky's face was reddish and swollen. Ham's too. Ham yawned a series of yawns opening his mouth to the widest.

'How do you like our staying together in this place, Pinky?'

She didn't answer. The morning had been lighting outside also inside a bit. She said, 'It is bright. The milk man goes ringing his bell.'

'Pinky, don't go near the window and show that you are here.'

She asked, 'What is time now?'

'Seven thirty, I should brush and have tea.'

'Wait, just wait. Two hours more, I feel sleepy.'

She moved over to a nearby chair, sat on, and dozed off. Hamilton visited the bookshelves one after another. Finally, went near the stand in a corner packed with Indian authors. Took out a volume, Arvind Ghosh. Placed it back, took out another. Rabindranath

Tagore. Placed it back, third one, Kushwant Singh. Placed it back. Hamilton asked himself, 'Why these people are so fond of beard?'

He went to the other side. Jawaharlal Nehru, Mulkraj Anand, R. K. Narayan. Good, all smart, clean shaven.

'Ham, I think it must be past nine.'

'Not past nine. Just nine.'

'Only half an hour more. Come away, away from there quickly. Switch off the fan. We will get ready. We will wait near the door and run out the moment the door is opened.' They went to the door side. Waited. Looking at each other pitiably.

'What we do, I think, is foolish, Ham. We shouldn't run out that way. We will be watched and stories will be spread, Ham. Listen, Let us hide ourselves. You, near the literature shelf, and me near philosophy shelf. Soon after opening, students will come here in groups. When they go, we will join and go along with them as if we had just entered.'

'Good idea, Pinky.'

As expected, door was opened in time. Students poured in groups, fresh and well dressed. Library got busy. Hamilton and Pinky Pop came out from hideouts. A four boy and two girl group was about go. Hamilton and Pinky Pop became one with them in no time and made their way out. And were going without knowing where.

'Ham, one minute.'

'What, Pinky?'

'Think for yourself, what is the use of going to police station and reporting to my uncle? That uncle is my close relative. If he comes to know of his incident, he will not keep quiet. He will tell it to everyone. I told you I am already engaged. I am going to my hostel. You?'

'If so, I am also going to my hostel.'

'Ham, I have to do a lot for preparing my thesis.'

'Pinky, just now it struck me. The afternoon first hour is Bennet Albert's. He will flay me alive if he doesn't see me in his class.'

'Okay, Ham. Forgetting whatever had happened, let us attend to our work. That is best. Good idea, isn't it? Bye.'

Chapter 79

The Food Compartments

Long ago, we were in cave. We were eating animals. Since in those days we didn't have pot, fire, and stove, we were eating them raw, all of us. Of course, before our birth.

We are post-cavemen born in post-cave era. Now, also, we eat animals, but not raw. We have our kitchen. There, we cook. Some post-cavemen have changed. After ages of consumption have, for some reason, averted animals.

Like in some families where all members do not belong to the same political party, all the members of the plant families do not adhere to their plant principle strictly. The plant men and the animal men do not keep their vow. The animal man eats plants, the plant man drinks animals, the drink that the plant man drinks doesn't come from the plant, it is yielded by the animals. The one who takes the boiled solid flesh is a non-vegetarian; and the one who takes the boiled liquid flesh is a vegetarian. That is how we have our classification on food.

In the business conferences, the conference halls are interspersed with the solid men and the liquid men. As they proceed to lunch, they separate and gather in their opted zones. Lunch progresses to the end when rows of ice cream stand on trays. There, the plant men and animal men reunite for a joint gobbling. The ice cream cubes pass into members of both the principles. The number of the cubes shoveled is counted, but not the cows and buffaloes that supplied the raw material to make the cubes.

According to us, to be a vegetarian, one can eat fodder; and the fodder-eating animals in liquid form. And one can eat corn; and the corn eating birds in solid form.

In Heber, the hatched chicks Hamilton eats in the non-vegetarian mess. The unhatched chicks Milton eats in vegetarian mess. It means Hamilton eats the bird. Milton, its egg, the laid egg goes into Milton, and the hatched egg into Hamilton. Both are eggs, also chicks.

Chapter 80

Man and Animal

In the cave days, the food style was the caveman ate animal, and the animal ate caveman. They ate each other mutually in order to survive jointly. The food of the one was in the life of the other. It is not a tit for tat. It was a necessity. Not an agreement, it was their way. Not a sacrifice, it is their designed relationship, though heartlessly heartless of the maker. It is hard to understand why it is not like not eating each other.

Originally, it was two-way. Now, it is one way. Only man eats animals. Animals are not allowed to eat man. If a man wants to have the taste of being eaten by an animal, what he should do? He should go to the central part of a jungle where tigers roam. If he is keen on tasting early, he should start out this very moment. He shouldn't delay. If he delays, and goes late, there will then be no tigers there. In their place will be villas and guest houses, lodges and cottages, theme parks and water games built to please the tourists.

Chapter 81

The Last But One

Hamilton's love for Heber is deep even today. Whenever the love is turned on, Hamilton visits his hall, which is half an hour drive on the Tambaram bypass. Once inside the campus, his boyhood memories crowd up. He drives slowly and stops at a spot near the quarters his professor lived. For stopping there, there is a reason.

One day, in his post-graduate second year, Hamilton was summoned to appear before his professor at his quarters. When he appeared, his professor did a least expected thing. He began to prophesy. What he prophesied about Hamilton came exactly true. It is to replay in his mind the professor's prophetic flashback and to enjoy its fun. Hamilton stops over there.

From the vehicle, he gets down, glances at the sky up, the ground below, and the trees around. Heber Hall at a stone's throw, he becomes a boy again. From there, one fast run covering the main hall, another run touching the hall rooms, he reaches the mess. There, he takes a juice of pineapple, famous in Heber.

In the mess, Hamilton makes a general enquiry. Then he rushes up to the photo gallery to his group photo first. In that stands Hamilton all spikes with his porcupine dark hair. He moves right gazing at the photos one by one. All seniors. He moves further on. There are the grand seniors—now in the world of eternal beyond from which no one returns. Heaving out a heavy sigh, Hamilton retraces and sees his own photo again. He moves left. Juniors. They have all taken to wings in the turns of their batches. Now, most of them should be with families, with kids, some with grand kids here and abroad, hopefully all Heber at heart.

Then dash up to the PG House. In two minutes, he is there, climb the steps. It is the first floor. Turn east, straight to the end, last but one. That was Hamilton's room. Two double three.

If open, peep in. There is a boy. Spend a few minutes with him, the tender young face with a long years to go to get coarsened by the outer world. Hamilton feels like kissing that boy for his being lucky to stay in that room, rest and study in it, sing and hum in it, think and scribble in it, dream and build castles in the air like Hamilton did about forty batches ago.

The boys of that room he met resembled Hamilton in many ways. In courage and timidity, in activeness and laziness, in clarity and confusion, in cool and hot temper, in seriousness and easy-going nature. But the real campus thrills, they didn't enjoy.

None did a night climb on the tree standing forlorn in the unfrequented precinct of the dark woodland, and watched the moonlit enchantment of the off-lying cricket ground. None did a midnight walk single to his classroom at the far end of the arts block, and from there to the wicket gate to see how it feels. All the same, the boy is the living thing of Heber, the budding thing of Heber, the future thing of Heber, somewhat of a similar thing of this Hamilton or some other Hamilton. What sort of Hamilton this boy would make? Way too early to tell that now. At the moment, an unweaned child in the arms of Heber.

During his visits, Hamilton found that the room had become smaller. Smaller? Not really. It is as it was.

While a student, the room's smallness, the cot's smallness, the rack's smallness, all these were not felt. He was under a spell, which had him lost in books.

At that time, Hamilton had not known that this little room was going to pave the way for his coveted destinations through sweet elevations punctuated by dramatic turns, the way studded with knowledgeable seniors, competent colleagues, and dynamic companions.

During his government days, to test his patience and talents, there was never a dearth of occasions. To manage those occasions, considerable work skill and managerial know-how were required. For those skills and know-how, his active extracurricular interests and organisational involvements shown in his hall were a good initiation.

The role that MCC played in his life is not small. It is with the great pride Hamilton acknowledges that he owes the positions occupied later sizably to Heber Hall that had excellent man-making facilities, and to his room that he used hermetically.

Part Four

Chapter 82

An All-Woman Mission

To the cosmic space, which is away, first went the machine. Then went the dog. And the last to go was man. Since the late last century, it has become a fashion of the countries, old or young, big or small, rich or poor, to launch spacecrafts giving worldwide publicity. Now, the explorations are male female combined.

Tell what is going to be the next move? An all-woman mission. That will indeed be great. But we can't say how it will end. We can only hope during the journey, the female astronauts would be friendly and not quarrel. How to find out if they are friendly or not? Instead of zooming straight toward its target, if their rocket tilts, we can guess that the quarrel has started. If the tilting increases, we can understand that the quarrel is getting worse. Then the control room will have to speak to the space women's boyfriends to intervene and to patch up.

The white man is fast. He has scored the highest number of visits. The yellow guy trails behind, while the brown chap has just begun his innings. The landed immigration was in the reverse order. The white man comes last. Before him, came the yellow guy following the brown chap. The colours didn't stay segregated long. When the colour pockets got full, they overflowed, intermixed, and brought forth new colours and new features. The present colour muddle and feature muddle came about only that way.

Now, it is hard to claim that a person is 100 per cent one geographically, one racially, one nationally, one culturally, or one linguistically. We don't know how many geographies, how many races, how many nations, how many cultures, and how many languages are inside a particular guy.

Chapter 83

Palace for Twenty Rupees

Who, under the sun, is not fond of a life of joy and freedom? An unquestioned life is always sweet. But you will not find it around where you live. To find that, you should get away, get far away, as far away as you can.

There are cities in India, especially the old ones, with interesting sites to see. Go to one of them you had never seen before, and there, hire a room. Not of a star luxury. The fellows who work there know nothing—nothing beyond catering. For them, the outer world is an unknown world. They can't understand your tastes and preferences. From them, you won't get any guidance that you want, much less from those who stay there. Among them who stay, there are two types: those who are on the way to earn, and those who are on the way to lose. They know only earning and losing, not being happy and free. The losers stay in gorgeous suites, which you should not book.

Take a room simple like in Heber. In the night hours, don't go out, watch no channel, browse no website. The senior room attendant is your guide. Collect all information from him about the city palace, which is the grandest among the oldest. In the morning, dress up well after a cold shower, only cold shower and no hot water. Have your breakfast and leave your room. Don't mind the distance, call no taxi, just walk. Now, you are walking toward history to see what the king has done for himself, his wives, and children.

Get into the palace as told to. Now, you are inside. Rightfully, that means you have bought that palace for twenty rupees at the ticket counter. It is yours now. You are its second owner till sunset. Move all over all places, all halls, all lanes, all corridors, and all corners. You may sneak into the room that is dark and cobwebbed, but light no torch. It will be a disturbance to the fly-away boy and girl making love there. Keep off bats.

Out in the open yard, sit on the bench under that banyan tree where the king and the queen sat for their evening breather. Lean on the back and take a nap on that bench, though not well-kept. Now, you are the king napping. In the nap, you may clean up and beautify your nap palace, and if you want, expand your nap kingdom and rule. After your nap ruling, open your eyes, get up, and move toward the gate—that huge one—huge enough to let an elephant in. Don't be shocked at the ill-smelling hills of cow dung, don't be offended at the throng of monkeys giving demonstrations of mischief, and don't be scared at the flights of pigeons descending from above to alight on your head. Stray out.

Pea nut or cucumber, Kurkure or ice cream, no matter what, buy and eat. Orange juice or buttermilk,

Coca Cola or Thumbs Up, drink and drink like a camel. Hygienic or unhygienic, never mind. Allow yourself freedom. Don't frustrate your tastes—the God given ones. Watch people keenly, greet the passers-by, chat with those who have some fun on their face, keep moving, purse safe, better to be always on the alert.

Outside that palace under a margosa tree, you will surely find an old man in rags. He may have been related to who was the king, his kingship usurped by the British, or possessions stripped by his concubine's secret lover. That old man is the one in need of a listener. You are the man he wants, and he is the man you want, your real professor of history with the living knowledge of a kingdom. He is dying with interest to tell you all—not the bald kind of headlines that you read in school texts and college notes. He will smile at you. Don't disappoint him, smile back. Go sit near him and listen. Time flies.

Now, how do you feel? You would feel that luckily, you were not that king. However, if you had been he, you would have managed the affairs of the kingdom better, and not have suffered so much. You would have hanged that unfaithful concubine and trampled her lover under the feet of a tusker. You would have put the complete collection of the palace women to death excepting the prettiest dance girl from Mexico.

History can be best heard and best enjoyed if you also could set your eye on such a man who could recount it with so much interest. To enjoy his tale, and to delight in a live history to the full, you know what you should do? You must go alone. Not with your wife.

Chapter 84

World War in Slow Motion

Cocks fight, monkeys fight, men fight, and also nations. If a war is fought within a nation, it is a civil war. If fought with another nation, it is an international war. If a number of nations fight, it is a world war. So far, we have fought thousands of civil wars, hundreds of international wars; but the world wars, only two.

In the third category, our performance is poor. We are just at one added to the lowest of the single digit. To make that three, we strive, but there is always some snag certain statesmen create. The major players don't take the lead. Instead of starting the war, they speak about peace. They speak about peace, and on the other hand, prepare for war also. Now, while the people are anxious about peace, we can't say they are wholly against war. The people want war also. They want to see how it starts, how it is fought, and how it ends. So when is then the third? We couldn't tell when. Maybe today or tomorrow or next month or next year or later. The world is waiting for it, sometimes patiently, sometimes impatiently.

Considering our war experiences, war interests, and war ammunitions we have developed, at least ten would be a good number—the lowest of the double digit. The world is war starved, it needs to be war comforted. But how to comfort? Let us comfort thus, 'Of course, we couldn't enjoy a bumper sort of war shots. Still, we are not unwise. We are fighting enough of wars. In mini-forms like the racial wars, terrorist wars, border wars, class wars, group wars, and street wars. In case even these wars fail, we fight our micro-wars like hotel wars, airport wars, train wars, bus wars, taxi wars, auto wars, and rowdy wars. In these wars, all the countries participate. These wars are fought some annually, some, biannually, some monthly some weekly, some daily, some every ten hours, some five hours, some two hours, some one hour, some half an hour, some every ten minutes, some five minutes, and some continuously. This is also a world war, though fought in bits and pieces.

The allied-axis world war kills in crores. These things kill in lakhs, thousands, hundreds, and tens. With this operating range of killing during the last half century of peace, if we could call it peace, we could have exceeded the total killing of both the world wars. It means we are fighting an undeclared third world war in slow motion. We live in a time of slow motion world war. This slow motion war is not a bad war, it is good, very good. We should like it since it is a war fought with the nuclear weapons at rest.

But the grievance is that the present war thrill is not satisfying. For a greater war satisfaction, what to do? Some suggest we can think of a pseudo war using robots—so many robots! From where to get them?

America, Russia, China, and Japan, the leading robot makers, will make and supply. But if robots fight, will it be like a real war? Will not be. In that, guns will not be fired, cannons will not rain shots, fighter jets will not bombard, cities will not be blown up, industries will not be shelled, fuel tanks will not explode, houses will not burn down, towers will not crash, electricity will not go off, darkness will not shroud, phones will not go dead, people will not die, and the earth will not become a graveyard.

The robot war will not be like a war at all. It won't be unlike the make-believe of Walt Disney. Then how to call that a war? Man's hunger is for real war only.

Chapter 85

Overnight Wonders

The leaders think, 'The war, if started, the consequences will be a disaster. Why start it in a hurry? Let us wait. At the same time, let us have the loaded gun ready to fire.'

The nations are willing to wound, but afraid to strike. They know if they strike first they can't escape the return shots. If those return shots hit their economy and put their nation to starve, then the people will not vote the leaders back to power. If the leaders force the people to support war, such a leadership will be internationally outlawed and the country economically stranded. The one who commences the action will have an exorbitant price to pay. Why start that hell in a haste? This is the question the leaders ask, a good question, the good saving question, saving single question. It is because of that question, we, in the world, still have our body and soul together. May that question live long!

The effects of wars have always been economically decisive. For one side, they were like a billion dollar lottery; and for the other, a virtual devastation. The centrifugal twist of wars in the past has shattered the established institutions. It has altered the owners of assets, and destroyed the proprieties of ventures. The present day ownerships of the hundreds and thousands of acres of land are the wonders wrought by wars, so are the ownerships of the massive palaces and prized estates. The movable wealth and the immovable assets are the windfalls of wars to the fortunate.

War transforms. It transforms the economic, social, and political maps. The existing maps are all, at the root, war-made.

War is a physical explosion of armed power for which there is no counterblast in the moral armoury. The post-war moves are conciliations, consolations, and compromises. They can't neutralise the effects of war. For the war-wounded people, healing may come in headloads of ants. For the war-raised lords, consolidation comes in shiploads.

Now, only this or that is what is going on in the world, nations, cities, towns, villages, and families too.

Chapter 86

The Angels and Devils

Of the people, the most thought about in the world fall into two groups: one, those who loved peace the most, two, those who loved war the most. The peace lovers give blood. The war lovers take blood. The blood givers are worshipped as angels. The blood takers are hated as devils. The top most human beings we read about in history are either these angels or these devils.

What makes a human being an angel? To find an answer is far above our heads. What makes a human being a devil? That, the scientists have discovered. A tumour.

After years of tireless research, the psychopathological analysts have brought to light that in a man diagnosed with war mania, there is a micro malignant growth in the epicenter of his brain constantly inducing choler.

Chapter 87

All Royal

The monarchical rulers had a consciousness. Irrespective of their places of rule, they considered themselves as one blood—one ruler blood. Even though at enmity, the rulers were one on vital relations.

Matrimonially, the rulers followed a single principle. The kings married the queens, and the queens married the kings. They never married below. The exceptions are not marriages, they are political eyewash left off to dissolve automatically.

The famous Indian rulers, known for their imperial glory, happily took for wives the women who were not of their clan, yet royal. The romantic princes of Naples readily took girls of Milanese descent, yet royal. The warlike kings of Rome had no problem in falling in love with and marrying the ladies of Egypt, yet royal. The crown prince of Norway chose for his life's partner a lady of Sweden, yet royal.

On the point of wedding, Greece and Italy were one, England and Scotland were one, Germany and France were one, Spain and Holland were one, Cooch Behar and Baroda were one, Wandhwash and Paris were one, Vellore and Ceylone were one—all royal.

Chapter 88

The Great

India, with its history so long, has scored to its credit only two kings as great—Asoka and Akbar.

Alexander would have easily become an Indian emperor had he not yielded to his soldiers who revolted to pull back. It is his bad luck that his ambition to extend his dominion to India ended as an untouched winning post. If it had not ended so, it would have added to India the credit of being ruled by another westerner history feels the proudest to call the great.

Chapter 89

Greatness Verified

On a weekend, late in the evening, an inquisitive team of ten history students walked into their professor's residence. The professor offered them a seat and asked, 'What is the matter with you, boys? What brought you here at this time of the day?'

'Sir, to seek a clarification.'

'What?'

'Sir, we would like to know on what basis certain kings are called the great?'

This was a doubt no one ever asked. After admiring the scholarly interest of his students exhaustively and sounding sweet almost to a fault, the professor excused himself, 'Okay, tomorrow we shall discuss in the class.' The team returned.

That night, the professor slept not a wink. He searched for the answer, which no book had. After pacing up and down like a caged tiger for some time, he grew weary. Early next morning when in dilemma, his common sense shook him up and chided, 'What a professor you are! You don't know even this! It is simple. I tell you what, listen, to qualify for Indian imperial greatness, the claimant should not be a woman, he should be a man. His name should start with *A*. He should be a king, should be good at horse ride, should have fought wars, cut heads, cut hands, cut legs, burnt houses, should have ruled India full or its major part. His father should have been a king, mother, a queen. He need not be tall, but should have some height. Should have a moustache in half the size of his head, turban, a must, and illiteracy, no bar. The extramarital status may be any high or any low. He should have generally fathered a large brood of kids, and through queens at least a few.'

Next day when the constituents of greatness were dwelt at length in the class by the professor, the students were amazed at the depth of his knowledge and begged him to reveal the source. The professor, unfastening his face into an august smile, told them, 'Why, for history, every one is a source. Even you, if you wish to be. The ten of you are ten learned sources.'

In the monarchical hierarchy, there are three levels: first, king; above that, emperor; at the top, great. Male greats in history are many like Ramses of Egypt, Sargon of Sumeria, Yu of China, Darius of Persia, and Alfred of England.

History has overlooked women. Cleopatra missed greatness. More surprisingly, Queen Elizabeth the first of Tudor. The overlooked list is lengthy, which includes the other queens like Himiko of Japan, Eleanor of France, Isabella of Spain, Mary of Scotland, Amina of Nigeria. Also Begum Sultana Razia, Rani

Lakshmi Bai of North India, and Queen Mangamma of South India.

History is biased. To mend it, feminists don't rise up in arms, they sleep. It would be good if someone rewrites history from a whole new female angle, calling at least one of the overlooked ladies, the Great.

Great was a royal prerogative. With the fall of monarchy, great also fell. It is not available for democratic adoption. The benchmark is mainly in how bloody the kings were, not so much in the good done. Mahatma Gandhi has done far more good to this country than any king, Sardar Patel conquered more kings than Asoka or Akbar, and Indira Gandhi followed it up waging an economic war against them and scored a resounding victory. But history didn't want them as great. It slammed the door of greatness on their face and bolted it fast inside.

There is no end to the number of those who fought and died to achieve greatness. So many fought, and so many died. But what did they mean by greatness? Not known clearly. Shall we define? It just means someone calling you great, believing it, you imagining all sorts of funny things about yourself.

Now, people have realised the emptiness of greatness. During the last twenty-five years, the meaning of the word great has undergone a sea change. Now, it conveys something diametrically opposite to its original meaning. It is working as a common adjective for where a better word to convey mockery could not be supplied by the dictionary.

Had Aristotle known about the degradation greatness would suffer, he would have advised Alexander not to fight wars, not to conquer kingdoms, not to suffer a high fever in Babylon, and there, not to die so young.

Chapter 90

Lord

Since great is an English word, the Englishmen did not want it to fall into disgrace. They have changed it into lord. To be raised into a lord is not hard. Simple. No need to be a king, or his son. No need to climb a horse or slay a man. No need to be an aristocrat or a scholar. No need to own a palace or an estate. Just a house in the semi-posh area, or one in a farm with a few fruit bearing trees will be enough. He can be a man of any calling, can be a politician, a courtier, a teacher, a poet, a soldier, a sailor, or a painter.

Chapter 91

Sir

The age of Lord gave birth to another age—the age of Sir. Sir is a formal word for salutation, the most used in English, the most used in the world.

Now, every male is a sir. We can't miss its courtesy if a business firm sends a message; its villainy, if a government man writes a throat-cutting letter demi-officially; or its beauty, if lisped softly by a Serbian air hostess, while on a long flight in a private airline.

Chapter 92

Shakespeare Also a Jew

In the colonial times, most Indians could dream of nothing beyond the next meal. Their thinking part could only idle. The utmost their brains could do was to echo what they heard, not understand. Their understanding is growing slowly. Now it has grown a little. With that little growth reached down the three centuries, they could understand certain basic truths like the Angles, Saxons, and Jutes were foreigners. If it grows a little more, they will understand the remaining truths like the French, Dutch, and Danish were also from the west.

To know those truths from, we have history, but that we read not for knowledge, only for academic compulsion; academic means reading in the month of April and forgetting in the month of May.

If you want to be a master of arts with least interest and no effort, do history. You will never fail. Anything you write is correct. If incorrect, it would not be brushed aside, it would make a point for research. If you say Emperor Asoka is not an Indian, but one who had come from Iceland, it will not be dismissed as nonsense. It will happily be accepted as an excellent thesis for a PhD.

History is not one. There are four histories in the world. One is what has already been written, another is what is being written. The third is what will be written, and the last is what will never be written.

There is generally a thinking that women don't write history. They write poems, novels, fictions, short stories, and scripts for screenplays. To journals and magazines, they write bundles and bundles of articles and snips. In the literary world, some of them are giants. Some young women are creatively more prolific than their writer mothers and writer grandmothers. Some who have turned ten years just twice have hit the world mark in literature. But the opinion that prevails is history, they don't write. In the library racks of history, there is a yawning feminine vacuum. It is often asked, 'Will anyone fill it?'

The modern women are not that much unenterprising. The fact is the vacuum has already been filled. There are women historians in hundreds and hundreds, for example, to put some alphabetically, Alice Garner, Barbara Harris, Carol Benedict, and Doris Goodwin. But the vacuum in the Indian libraries is slow to fill.

In the early days, women were shy. They didn't like to come out to the open as women, they came out in the guise of men. They did so in many fields including the field of letters. Among such women, it is said that one is Amelia Bassano Lanier. Who is that? A Jewish she who had passed for an English he. Which English he? Shakespeare. We have to wonder if there is really anything that people will not say or will not do. Who knows tomorrow someone might concoct a piece of evidence and try to make out that Shakespeare is also a Jew!

Chapter 93

The Unloving Trash

This is my country. That is your country. I am this, you are that . . . I am this, you are that . . . I am this, you are that . . . I am this, you are that. To speak so is nothing but bullshitting, an unhealthy consciousness of something that makes one human being different from another. Hell with that rot.

What are countries? Countries are chance entities. The countries could not have been there on the world map had history taken another route. The countries are man-made, but people are the creation of the almighty, a perfect creation, perfect in form, perfect in look, perfect in beauty, not like their countries. See the shapes of the countries, see their border edges. There is nothing beautiful, nothing proportioned.

They conform not to any of the geometrical patterns. No country is a perfect round, a perfect square, a perfect triangle, a perfect rectangle, or a perfect rhombus. Their borderlines have no rhyme, no reason. They are like drawings drawn by monkeys.

Human beings have a definite structure, a definite look. To say that a man is a man and a woman is a woman, we don't have to look at them twice whatever be their country, or the way they have dressed.

The people are God-made, they are divine. What is divine has a universal right. They should not be tied down to what are known as their native lands. The world is a park, the whole world, which all are entitled at least to visit freely. The world is our home, and the things in it are ours. They are for our pleasure. But human minds are narrow. When a thought hardens into an unalterable frame of mind, it discounts generous notions and rational outlook. The idea of a nation is but the settled narrowness of our intolerant nature.

Chapter 94

Man the Destroyer

Man is a weird creature. He won't accept a thing as a thing. He would make it into a problem, and would want to see it as one. His nature is to turn any parkland into a wilderness, and enjoy the pleasure of getting lost into that. What is straight or open, bright or beautiful cannot exist as such with him. He is sure about nothing, steady about nothing, and clear about nothing. He is caught in a sort of confusion.

Watch the animals. With them, there is no confusion whatsoever. They are clear, they know what they need—to live happily. Their needs are specified. For them, the wood is their home, the land is their playground, the river is their pool. For the carnivorous animals, the living beings that move about are their food. For the herbivorous animals, their food is in the living things that stand fixed on the earth.

Plants do not eat animals or birds. They don't want them for anything. Heaven is there to rain them food. They want the earth only to stand on.

No animal wants a human being the way man wants it. Man wants animals, some for meat and milk, some for bone and blood, some for skin and wool, some for dung and urine, some to catch, put in a cage, and play with, and some to see from a distance and marvel at their appearance. No bird wants a human being the way man wants it, but man wants all birds for the purposes we know.

Man is nothing if not a destroyer. He is destroyer from nature's point of view, from animal's point of view, from bird's point of view, and, of late, from his own point of view. He is therefore the hated foe of nature, animals, birds, and himself.

Man wants the whole universe without omitting any of its parts, but nothing in the universe wants man, neither the animate nor the inanimate. The most unwanted thing among all the creations of God is man. Man is more than beastly. He wants first of all to eat up things. If alone, eating is possible, he would have long ago wolfed down the whole earth like it is the Punjabi fried chicken.

Since eating is not possible, he puts it to various other uses. Where the other uses are also not possible, he mars it. But to this day, no amount of marring has satisfied him.

More than half the birds, he has shot; half the animals, he has killed; half the forest, he has cut; and half the earth, he has dug. Human beings are like a swarm of termites surrounding the earth. They are biting the earth to bits, and spitting the bitten bits away.

Nothing in the world would be safe so long as man lives on it.

If the evolution had progressed not beyond monkeys, the earth would have been a heaven.

Chapter 95

A Burning Ball of Fire

The countries are busy. So much not working toward peace and prosperity as toward starting a war or resisting it. To start or to resist, they are either equipping themselves or seeking to lean on those already equipped. Surely, at an unexpected moment, they would start their fun, their great bomb fun of turning the earth into a burning ball of fire.

Fun has two parts: one, the fun itself; another, its after talk. Without the after talk, the enjoyment of the fun would be incomplete. But in the case of bomb fun, for an after talk, it will be too late. Here, we neither watch nor comment. Is there a way to enjoy them both? Yes, there is.

A mock bombing can be added to the Independence Day agenda. That can be programmed as the climax of the celebration at the national, state, and district headquarters. It will be not only an entertainment, also an enlightenment. It will give us an idea as to how we are being meant to get finished.

At the end of the Independence Day mock bombing, in their after talk, people would raise a hundred doubts including, 'Do these nuclear things have a life span? Will they get old and then get too old to explode? Can they be diffused like the country bombs are by the policemen? Can we put them in a heap and set them on fire? Can we not dump them in the Antarctic Ocean for the fish to eat up and to die vicariously?'

Where do they keep them now, down in the ground or up in the air? Is there any maintenance for them? How they dust? Using vacuum cleaners? How often they grease? Daily? Weekly? Monthly? Or annually, once for the inspection of the major general?

These weapons are dangerous. They are intended to finish the enemies. They should not finish our own men accidentally. It is hoped they should be under some strong security, and always under lock and key. Here, the key is the most important. Who would have it? The army chief or the operator boy? The supreme commander or the gatekeeper? It will be good if the key is not misplaced or lost. If the fighting mechanism is computer operated, there would be a password, which must be a secret. As it is a secret, we all have a duty. We should pray. Pray what? Pray that it should be truly a secret.

Chapter 96

The Disarmament

Most nations keep their silence. Strangely, the nuclear ones don't. They are noisy. Noisy about what? Disarmament.

What is disarmament? Disbanding the war men? Closing the ordnance factories? Stopping production? Freezing the stockpile of weapons? Winding up research? Reducing the sale of arms? Clipping down the defense budget? Surrendering weapons?

Our disarmament would never be a success because there is so much confusion about what it is. If we want that to mean surrendering weapons voluntarily, it is funny. Who will surrender? Not one. If any nation comes forward to, it may surrender, but never the whole stock. It would keep the best behind its back.

We have been hearing like, 'We would hit back if hit.' What is important is the hit starters should be stopped from starting. Before that, they should be stopped from having with what they would start. And much before that, they should be stopped from entertaining the very thought of starting.

The last is not a light job. For that, the top heads, instead of sitting pretty in their home states all their life, should come out and meet the other heads. Meet more often, say, at least twice a year. Discuss matters affecting the nations threadbare and reach solutions. When the meeting has ended, they shouldn't fly back the next second. They should halt a couple of days in a common guest house. And there, like good friends, play some game, and have some fun. Then the friendship, began at the head level, will percolate down to their people.

The best place for such summits is the world's most intelligent nation—the Vatican City, which has no president, no prime minister, no army, no navy, no air force, no SSM, SLBM, SRBM, ICBM, even no land more than half square kilometres. Yet, how peaceful and how prosperous!

A leader to leader, face to face, mind to mind, and heart to heart get together will iron out the differences and foster the spirit of oneness.

Ages of our living have gone meaningless, they have not taught us how to live in peace. We are still learning. In future, we will have so much to learn that we can only learn. To live what we have learnt, there will be neither interest nor scope.

Poor planet, poor politicians, poor nuclearists, poor terrorists, and poor us. We are doing our works, given or chosen, without knowing what the next minute is going to be like. It is funny that we exist, all of us, to come to naught together the moment something inside a crazy head goes awry.

The terrorist onset is not like an air crash, bus collision, or boat capsize that occurs by oversight. It is a meticulously planned criminal conspiracy. It finishes life, ruins assets, disturbs peace, and spreads panic sometimes to an immeasurable extent.

To prevail over, ingenious strategies are being tried out. But they've got us nowhere. As an alternative, an all-world hunter force may be formed. This can comb the hideouts, round up and bring the terror men to a spot. Not for anything else, but to teach them a lesson. A lesson on the virtues of peace and harmony that Mahatma Gandhi stood for hoping we too would follow.

Chapter 97

The Last Holiday

If the Gandhian lesson goes up as vapour, and if the disaster is sure to strike, then we will have no way but to weep. But should we weep? Weep really? To weep is silly. The calamity will strike when it will strike. To strike, let it take its time. In the mean while, why should we weep? Let us plan out something. What to plan? There's nothing to stop the nuclear thunder or the terrorist storming. These are beyond our power. And so what? A Fun, a good fun. Rather, a long fun. We shall have that fun, not a small fun. A great fun, not a home fun, not a club fun or Heber fun, not a localised thing. A world fun, not just for an hour, not for a day, not a week, not a month. That is too short. It can be much longer.

We, the humans, are joyless beings. Since the first man set foot on the earth, we have had nothing like a lasting joy. We shall have that now.

Before accomplishing our nuclear self-hanging, let us forget ourselves in a recreation. We all know, without spending money, there is no joy in the world. Let us therefore spend all that we have. One full year, we will do no work, go nowhere, at our own place or the places we like, with our near and dear, we will enjoy a year-long fun, a year-long spending spree.

If you have no money, no need to worry. Take a loan. These days, the banks give readily. See that it is a huge loan—minimum of one hundred and twenty lakhs of rupees. Call it your fun loan and spend at ten lakhs a month. It is an open fun. All of us all over the world including the state heads can take part. You can enjoy whichever pleasure you choose, and in whatever manner you like. But it should be a true enjoyment. It can be a year of special love, special friendship, special happiness, special everything. At the end of the one year revelry, the one year great revelry, the countries can do one thing—one great thing—hard to agree though.

What is that? They can all open upon themselves the whole stock of their own bombs on a commonly agreed day or a commonly agreed night or at the stroke of commonly agreed midnight. And thus, close the human part of the world's story. A closing preceded with the grandest live audio-visual extravaganza! This would show how extraordinary we, the human beings, are, capable of conceiving such an end.

Many may take exception to this idea and pooh-pooh it as idiotic. But Hamilton would hold his ground. Would defend it with all his conviction and assert it as wise, quite wise. As much wiser than all on a sudden getting torn to pieces, leaving all our earnings, savings, and assets to be turned into ashes like it happened in Japan when Hamilton was 1 year old.

Chapter 98

Only Women Know That

There had been turns in history, and one of them was a miracle. It saved us from the face of Mr Bullet. Mr Bullet's military short sight revolved immediately 360 degrees around; his far sight, 40 degrees eastward, and zero degree far southeast.

It appears providential that India, which had been the common butt of western hit, failed to draw his attention. Having brought the whole of Europe under his moustache, the poor man fell in love with a wrong lady—Russia. He made a passionate advance to kiss her, but was repulsed grievously. Mr Bullet had taken no counsel from the past and learnt nothing from the lesson that his wrong lady had taught to Mr Helena.

It is known full well that Mr Bullet was a school dropout. Fiery speeches and hot battling were his fortes. He was vengeful and a hope high. But that hope didn't work, it failed. When it had failed him and he begun to realise that he had no life to live, Mr Bullet got married at four years to sixty, and that was only to leave this world bride and groom within hours of their union.

Mr Bullet died and the world escaped. His country took years to recover from the war jolt. The results of the Second World War would have been cataclysmic for us had Mr Bullet given a cold stare to Russia and cast a loving smile on India.

We have men in history. Among them who sat on certain power seats and visited certain war fields are the milestones. The recent milestones are Mr Plassey, Mr Helena, and Mr Bullet. These milestones know nothing of love. Military academies and battlefields had taught them only hatred. These people were lordly with the least understanding of what is beautiful in human sense. They don't know what good humour is. They never shared a breezy moment the way we do. There had been nothing good, nothing sweet, or nothing tender about them. All just ferocity.

What's surprising is even after them, women ran. Not just ran, also loved. Not just loved, also married. How difficult are women to understand? What actually is that which they like in men? Of course, not an easy question to answer. But history has proof to show that they can like even such men who, in cold blood, sprayed bullets into the heads and chests of their fellow men. If they hadn't liked applying their micro-soft touch and the macro-tantalizing smile, they would've tamed their men and brought them into natural love. They didn't tame. They perhaps thought, 'Nothing would be wrong if my husband does.'

Some writers aver that it is these women who incited their fiendishness. They rubbed them on the wrong side at wrong times. Mrs Plassey threatened to sail back to England, giving her guards a slip, while her man was in the thick of his battle. Mrs Helena provoked her little corporal by slighting his gallantry when toying with his dream of world empire. Mrs Bullet revealed her shock curtly over the irregular teeth of her hubby when giggling with Goebbels.

These incidents show one thing clearly. What? Men have gone berserk where their women held them not within their gravitational limit. Because the women had let their husbands loose, their husbands were unleashing their savagery on others.

History is hasty, often erring ineptly in judgement. It has the habit of bestowing eminence on whoever comes in its view. It treats no one as small, no one as bad. It is stone-blind to their moral side. All that history wants is slaughter, and someone to cause it, so that there can be a shedder of the blood and a history of the world.

Tell who will be the tomorrow's world hero. Not a gentleman president, not a dedicated prime minister. For that status, the historians would choose only a terrorist because it is he who comes in the historical bloody line.

History is born on blood, and marches on to shed more and more of it. On its pages, there is no appreciation of moderateness or criticism of excesses. When excesses have crossed limits, history would not rebuke, it would glorify. To be great in history, one should be bloody; to be the greatest, the bloodiest. In the course of world history in so many contexts, for the worst of the blood guilty, you can hear tributes like a great warrior, a brilliant strategist, a military genius, a tiger in action, a lion-hearted adventurer.

If we could take a calm few minutes and think, we will not hesitate to conclude:

'Had there been a healthy law governing the whole world, under it, several of the great war heroes could have been judged as criminals and hanged.

Chapter 99

Assassinations

A great leader of a great country fought for his nation. His great killer of the same country fought for his reason. Both fought, both won, both achieved their goals, both their names came out in the newspapers. Later entered history books, the first letter of their name parts respectfully in capital.

In the history books, they are in the same page, in the same paragraph, in the same sentence. In the monument of that one sentence, they sleep side by side lying at a point-blank range.

The above is not just a nameless narrative, it is a format. You can fill up the blanks with the applicable names relating to various countries. If you want to do a comprehensive job, over one hundred formats will be required to cover all the nations in which leaders had been martyred.

The bloodier the country, the greater the killing. Each country has an inner darkness, which can be scanned through the kind of killers and the causes of the killing. The killers are not always men. There are women also. But the male female ratio is not one is to one.

Chapter 100

Family Planning

The early man had a huge flock of children. His children were cavefull and hillfull. But many of the countries in modern days want children not to be so many. They have got future conscious and are not prepared to risk their countries to excess population. So for the computer chap, the advice given is, 'Limit your children to one or two.'

These countries have beautifully standardised their family size through a method called family planning. What is family planning actually?

First, it is a confession—the governments' confession—that they can't manage their countries if the people have more than two children for a couple. Then it is a drive to ensure that the population doesn't exceed their capacity to feed.

Countries want animals to populate and humans to deplete. Animal births, they welcome; human births, they abhor. They are afraid of children, afraid that a child born is a threat to their resources. A rat in the warehouse godown, so they are obstructing the child production in as many ways and at as many points as they can.

Minute to minute births are flashed at the city traffic signals. Those in the vehicles count the number, note the additions, and wonder, 'How fast are men!' But what do the additions want us to do? Should we plead guilty to the extent we had been personally fast ourselves? Should we implore our fellows to go slow? Or should we keep seeing the electronic displayer absent-mindedly till ploughed into by the vehicle at the back?

Man is born. Having been born, he is preventing births. The only interest sure in all men is to help the births to go on. Since it is dangerously sure with the men of certain countries, check is felt exigent. Having understood the exigency, the governments, in their anxiety, are distributing the birth prevention appliances. All in need take them and use. The schoolboys and the schoolgirls too.

Chapter 101

Flavoured Oxygen

Science has been helping us in a thousand ways, but all the helps are not wholesome. Some create side effects. The worst of the side effects science has created is it has pumped out the element we need for breathing. Now, the air in the sky has no oxygen. The oxygenless air is causing in us changes.

Among the changes it is causing, one is the discolouring of skin. Over a period, all the humans will lose their colour and become dark. The traces of that change are discernable, it is told.

One day, people all the world over will be single pigmented. No colour races, no colour distinctions, no colour strife. We will all be of one skin dye. And then what? On the dark skin, hair will grow. Dark skin and over it, dark hair, thick and shaggy hanging from head to foot. Furthermore, as days pass, feature changes will manifest. In appearance, the humankind will degrade into another. And that will be the kind close to what stands at our back according to the theory of evolution.

The rest is for Darwin to deal with, but Darwin cannot. He had propounded evolution. But here, it is devolution, it's opposite. He can't debunk his own discovery.

Right from when science came, we have been abusing the surroundings with toxic wastes. Most of what we consume are reaching us, having left poison on their way, in the three states: solid, liquid, and gas. The solid goes to the earth, the liquid goes to the water, and the gas goes to the air. Finally, all the three go into us through the mouth and the nose. The earth is supplying poison to eat, water is supplying poison to drink, and air is supplying poison to breathe. Our intake, therefore, in any form is poison.

The side effects of our scientific inventions have transgressed all bounds. Now, we are close to reaching the point of no return. What to do? We may perhaps try to arrest the side effects. To arrest the side effects, large-scale damage control measures will have to be taken. What kind of damage control? Couldn't be found out.

When in a tight corner, to help us out, we always have our businessmen. They will not just watch, they know how to capitalise on our helplessness. Soon, they will put up factories and produce the breathing air. The skyline will be a multi-coloured milky way of the ads of air blazing forth their brands as pure oxygen, flavoured oxygen, double life oxygen, oxygen Eden, oxygen Zion, and oxygen China.

Presently, we live protected by the immunity inherited from our ancestors. Once the market takes over our air needs, our immunity will leave. When immunity leaves us, we will be susceptible to the attack of all sorts of viruses and germs. The affected human trunks will launch the infection missiles in all directions. The epidemics would break out through swine and rats. When epidemics break out, the situation would go the whole lot worse. The world will become one of incurable ills and unchecked deaths.

Then where is our refuge? Nowhere else. We have only the bazaar to fall back upon. Its oxygen apparatus will form a part of our body, nose with a tube connecting a container hanging on our back. That, we will wear, all of us. It will be a daily 24x60x60 second wearing. Once we play into the hands of the oxygen traders, there will be no breaking away. We will be writhing in discomfort as their life-long captives.

We know market to function requires certain auxiliary supports. The most important, the transport, but no transport is reliable. It is infamous for going off-road at crucial junctures. If the transport strikes work, if the distribution boys reach us not in time, and if the delivery of oxygen is delayed, what next? Suffocation. The suffocation if extended, what? The end. When the end nears, the victims like the fish out of water will twist, wriggle, roll into a coil, and fall off still with the eyeballs thrust out.

Before that, if there is time for help from above, we will fall on knees, lift up hands, and cry, 'Oh, God! The gracious almighty! May the man-made life supports not fail! Heavenly father, let the transport strike be called off. Good Master, Godspeed the oxygen boys and have mercy upon us. Amen.'

Chapter 102

One Fine Morning

That principal was a good man, himself a student of English Literature from Madras Christian College. He had known Hamilton from his pre-university days, and been watching his academic progress stage by stage.

Having heard that Hamilton had written his MA, when that principal sent for him, Hamilton went. When he went, he was stunned at the hugeness of the hope that the principal had about his passing. As an evidence of his hope, the principal offered Hamilton an undated appointment as assistant professor of English to take effect from the day of his result.

As said, Hamilton's MCC professor, about a couple of years ago, had given him prophecies, which were to come true one by one. Hamilton guessed the offer of this teaching job was the fulfillment of the first. While offering the job, the principal made a request to Hamilton not to leave the college in the middle of the year if he gets a better job. Hamilton further guessed if he got a better job, and had to leave the college in the middle of the year, it would be the fulfillment of the second.

He did get a better job. Since it was a real better job for which he had been selected through a service commission, the principal could not stop him from leaving. Duly relieved, he did leave that college right in the middle of the year. Not long after leaving, great things started happening. The new job raised Hamilton to several high profile positions. One fine morning, the collector and district magistrate; the second fine morning, the director in a ministry; the third fine morning, the chairman of an industrial establishment; the fourth fine morning, the revenue commissioner at Madras; the fifth fine morning, a delegated spokesman at Delhi; and another fine morning, an official signatory abroad.

Chapter 103

The Worst a Man Can Do

How man began his life? He began his life with killing. First, he killed animals; next, birds; and last, his fellow men. To kill his fellow men, he used multifarious techniques. One of them was the technique of poisonous gas. The first man who used this gas technique is Hitler. Even if someone else had done that earlier, let us overrule history and give that credit only to the German Fuhrer. He is the right man for the place of first because it is he who, according to Judith Morgan, had 'just got mad', did the killing, and bunged the dead into the grave so cruelly.

Hitler carried out the gas killing in his concentration camp on the race of outstanding intellect. An incomparable human class, it is acting as the pillar of power and prosperity of the nations that are economically vibrant. Hitler's death carnage is an unprecedented explosion of racial aversion.

Thank God, Hitler is no more. He is dead. He died a death, which was sudden and desperate. He is the greatest of the world figures to die on a self-shot. We believe that the gun he used is the mightiest ever. If available on sale, any gun-crazy hobbyist, whatever the cost, would immediately buy and treasure it securely in his showcase. Others would like at least to see. It is the weapon that has killed such an atypical man. If auctioned, it will fetch Germany a billion deutsche marks. If not auctioned, just for that one gun, an exhibition can be opened at Berlin. If opened, it would be a great tourist excitement attracting ten times more visitors than Martin Luther King's burial site in Atlanta, Lincoln's Cemetery in Spring Field, or Gandhi's Samadhi in Delhi.

It is said, inside a man there is a ghost, which is no other than himself in spirit form. After death, it comes out and acts. Acts invisibly. How would the Hitler's ghost be and how would it act? Certainly, it would not be like the one of an average mortal. It would think terribly and act with a plan—a great plan of destruction. First, it would open its gas on its own countrymen for having given it up when encountering a setback. Next on Russia, for its nerve to come as close as to its very bunker, next on its axis neighbour who was of little help to it when it was at its wit's end. And then it would turn on the rest of Europe, one country after another.

Poor ghost. We don't know how it would finish the US. The US, as a precaution, would cover the whole of itself with a gasproof dome, and over it, spread a bombproof security umbrella.

America knows what bombing is. It has dropped two bombs each in power 20,000 Tons of TNT. It knows when its little boy jumped down on Japan, how that country went up in flames, and how Pilot Paul enjoyed the sight of the giant sized 45,000 feet high smoke mushroom that emerged from the explosion. The USA is fast. It knows how to stall such a thing from happening to it.

Hitler was a terror. While alive, about him, books were not written because they were afraid to be. After making sure that Hitler was not around, one man made bold to write. He is Nostradamus, a French Jew, an occult genius, a seer into the future. Hamilton looked up the prophetic piece of Nostradamus for Hitler's ghost. It is there, identifiably there, with the name of Hisler's shadow. There are other mentions also, but they make us no sense. Of course, it is not Nostradamus' fault. We lack grasp. We feel, 'It would have been easier to grasp if this man, Nostradamus, had written his prophesies in plain prose directly in English. But there is a trouble. English and prophecy don't go together. No Englishman was ever a prophet. None said what the future would be like. If an Englishman had foretold the fate of the British imperialism, England would probably have had its heart and mind turned to improve the lot of its own people.

Most of who said about the future are the Indian Vedic Aryans, the pyramid time Egyptians, the Jews of pre and post Christian eras, the great Islamic, and the Chinese prophets.

The French text of Nostradamus, rendered into English quatrains, is too difficult for any brain to penetrate. The Jews have a bad habit. Always. They all the time think, think of the difficult things, discover difficult things, and tell those difficult things in a difficult way. Sigmund Freud, people don't understand still. Einstein, to be understood, took a quarter of a century. Karl Marx, the whole of his lifetime eluded human understanding.

Nostradamus is the most complex. To understand him takes a fervid interest and a prodigious effort. Before opening his pages for the knowledge of the past, we should have read the world history countrywise and warwise, kingwise and assassinwise, queenwise and paramourwise. We should have known science, mainly astronomy, cosmology, oceanography, and seismology. For the knowledge of the future, we should have known the scriptures of Hinduism, Judaism, Christianity, and Islam. And have deeply read the Revelation of Saint John the Divine in the new testament of the Bible chapterwise, incidentwise, and imagerywise.

Saint John and Nortradamus share several visions, not to mention the vision of rapture.

During the second world war, Nostradamus' was the most read work among the world leaders including Churchill. The leaders burnt volts and volts of midnight electricity over the predictions as to how the war would end. Hitler too.

Hitler was angry with Nostradamus. He would have hijacked the prophet in his Nazi Aircraft Horten 2—29, and put him to gas death at his war camp for not forecasting him a century long world dictatorship. Hitler couldn't do that. Nostradamus had already died a gentleman's death in France four hundred years before Hitler died his Smith and Wesson Serial 709 death in Germany.

Chapter 104

Terrorism - 2

Now in the world, for any public mishap, the first cause suspected is terrorism. There is no symptom that terrorism would soften or thin out. It just grows, defies, defies outright. We hear its large-scale operations. We hear them from the national capitals in the broad daylight killing thousands. We hear also its small-scale operations. We hear them from the miniature hamlets under the cover of night, killing hundreds, pulling down huts, extorting people, and like a phantom bolting out with whatever falls to its shake.

Our security is mediocre. Couldn't rise up to its task. Consequence? The people are dying before their times. This is saddening. Worse still, enraged by frustration or enticed by gain, the youngsters pledge their loyalty to the terrorists.

The governments think of cracking terrorism through challenge, but challenge doesn't pay, it only stiffens resistance and aggravates hostility. Terrorism is proving to be too tough to be addressed either by force or by reason. It is a set of voices and sudden actions. It has no law, yet it has a will. Will to do what? A puzzle.

In any place with a crowd of one thousand people, at least one is expected to be a terror man. There, if an unclaimed something is spotted to the law enforcing authority, an alarm is given. In thirty minutes, arrives the sniffer dog to check it inside out for a bomb.

Terrorism is not a nation to nation problem, not a government to government problem, not a people to people problem, also not a cross issue. Not possible to spell out what. It is said that it works backed by private benefactors of high invisibility.

Our terror handling styles are funny. The US sends a troop of its army. India watches it curiously, as if it is the only thing it should do. Pakistan, already a worried nation, knows only to get more worried. For China, terrorism is not an issue. It is a light comedy played by certain froward lads miles away from their great wall. For other countries, it is not yet a problem, but they know what terrorism is. So they choose to lie low to safeguard their glass house of peace and comfort.

India has been receiving blow after blow. The US has been receiving threats mixed with blows—blows once in a while, threats, daily.

Some nations often caution the world that the terrorists are turning nuclear. They also send warnings that the terrorists might turn thieves and tiptoe off with the nuclear explosives, and for that, they are waiting for when the guard of the nuclear yard might snooze.

Each time a nation cautions so, its leader grows two inches in the height of his international popularity. For a national leader to polish up his popularity today, the shortest way is to say something about the terrorists and their bomb plans. The American presidents know how to keep their image luminous by every now and then spreading their terror guesses across the world.

Next, after popularity in guessing the terror minds, is India. China is least interested in this sort of dramatics. It wants its time for its business. Its main business is its own business, its own business on hand. What is it? To keep itself strong, strong in all fields, especially in the military to thwart the threat attempt, if any. It doesn't waste its time on fantasies. That the terrorists know. They also know that they can't withstand if the Chinese dragon gets wild, but it will not get wild for fun; it is a mellowed dragon, for its land area, population bulk, army strength, space feats, and economic speed, it is incredibly quiet.

America, India, and Pakistan are under a mounting pressure to get terror free. Whenever they apprehend a terror repetition on them, they get soft and their concern for human safety expands worldwide.

Chapter 105

The Greater Threat

The warlike nations are always innovative in evolving ways to destroy. They are evolving ways to cause the greatest destruction in the shortest time. The shortest way, they have evolved, is the nuclear way. According to the latest war fashion, not to be nuclear is to be militarily a lame duck.

Presently, there are two nuclearisms. One is in the hands of the terrorists—that we may call terrorist nuclearism. Another is in the hands of the states—that we may call state nuclearism. The terrorist nuclearism is in its infancy. It has to grow by stealing rather than making. Its danger level can be guessed somewhat.

The state nuclearism is with the leaders who are stocking their inventions behind the curtain. Their danger level is not guessable. We may therefore call the one as guessable nuclearism, and the other as unguessable nuclearism. All the nuclear nations fall under the unguessable category. The unguessable things are worse than the guessable things because they are intended for total extermination in an action of a minute.

These bomb hoarders only speak about the nuclear dangers, not the others. The others are just minding their business as ever, probably thinking, 'Well. In the feared nuclear suicide, let all the bomb fools kill themselves first. We shall enjoy life to the last penny in the pocket. When we are done with that last penny, we shall decide what to do. Join the suicide or flee.'

The nuclear nations now look innocent like the cockroaches. But they would not be the same when they break into offensive fits. They would breathe out fire like the legendary Leviathan.

To make the innocent looking cockroaches really innocent, we need someone who has an enormous human understanding and enormous human appeal like Mahatma Gandhi had. He should regard the world as his own, the whole world; the nations as his own, all the nations; and the people as his own, all the people.

For such a soul, the terrorists would appear not as terrorists. They would be an erring band of spoiled playboys. He would go straight into their camp, sit in their midst, and smile his proverbial smile broad into their face. Before that mesmerizing smile of love, terrorism can't stand. It will blush and roll back.

Gandhi could make the greatest thing happen to his nation peacefully because he was not an army man, not a government man, not a private man. He was a man, an example for the wisest man who had understood the value of peace and the power of conscience. Honest and dynamic, bold and determined, he was the product of India, its beauty, and its need.

A half clad frail man, an answer to an imperialism. He is the first liberator who liberated a nation from the clutches of the foreigners without resorting to bloodshed.

Gandhi led his own people after championing the cause of the victims of a similar oppression in South Africa. He opposed oppression, not the oppressors. Instead, he loved them. He was an extraordinary human being with an undefeated confidence in the good nature of man. Majestic in simplicity, all love at heart, he showed the world the best a man could do for the good of his fellow men in the most non-violent way.

Some equated him with Jesus Christ. And Indira Gandhi hoped he would resurrect. One of the greatest personalities history produced, he is gone, gone leaving us behind to keep wondering about him till the megacosm will cease to be.

The politicians, too, could be saintly. For that, Gandhi is a testimony. We now want one like him, the leader of the cause, the cause of overpowering terrorism and nuclearism, also the latest other -isms like chemicalism, biologism, and virusism by a weapon unknown to others. That bloodless, yet the invincible weapon of love, a man with the vision of Gandhi alone knows.

We have leaders for sections, for classes, for races, and for nations. But no leader for all put together. There is no leader in the world to take up the threat issues with the unflinching dedication. We need a leader. But him, we can neither make nor elect. The real world leader, only God should give. We don't know when he will. Till he sends us one from heaven, we will have no way but to wail.

Any remedy? No remedy. Only escapes.

One: Forgetting.
Two: Compromising
Three: Dreaming

Why dreaming at last? Dreaming is all we can do, the helpless people in the world.

Life has emptied its charm, reality tastes bitter, the world of man's making has let him down. Man, as a collective body, didn't do well. He is a collective failure, a collective fear. Now, he is a collective danger posing a threat of collective end. No wonder to pass over the state of despondency, man is in sore need of an unreal world—an unreal world to rest in and unreal people to rest with. So he seeks dreams in which to find an unreal life.

The threat stands like a monster armed from head to toe. We will have to live in future more and more narrowly expecting every second the abhorred thing to strike.

Let us therefore seek a dream daily once. In that dream world, we can all speak and listen to one another, sing and rejoice with one another, also cry to one another about how much we feel plagued. For a joint dream, we want a convergence. A well meant healthy one.

It is not a physical convergence. That is not possible, not a political convergence. That is useless, a convergence in dream, a waking dream with the waking dream people—the easiest to desire. In the dream convergence, we can feel that every nation is everybody's, and everyone belongs to everyone else. What a good convergence! An imaginary great convergence, a foolish one though.

A daily meet in the evening to realise the dream of all for goodwill is bound to reward in its own way.

This meet, which is a transcendental interfusion of hearts, is not in a single man's hand, but is possible with spontaneous association of all. It just needs us to volunteer to unite; unite in spirit from wherever we are.

For that, it is not money we need. In fact, it is the one that played us the devil. Hamilton is speaking not about what is possible with money, but about what is possible absolutely without it. Not money, just a little of our time that you spend. Spend it in the words of Omar Ghayyam, 'Before we, too, into the dust descend.'

Chapter 106

The Dream March

Now, when the political part and the terrorist part of humanity are contemplating a nuclear game of ruin and disaster, let us play a joyous game of peace and unity, fun and forgiveness. If the world still lives, it lives on two things. Tolerance and forgiveness. Certainly not on vengeance and vindictiveness.

To begin with, may we spare daily a time of fifteen minutes? This is for opening the hearts for love to flow and to fill us all. Fifteen minutes of inter-blood emotional identification with one and all in a happy world of waking dream.

Imagine, or if possible, place a globe at the centre of those around. Fix your place on that. You are in two places at the same time now. One, your family world; another, your world family. Roll the globe. The toy globe that we roll and the real globe that God rolls meet. In that meeting, we merge all the people into one.

You are one of all people taking the floor for a dance in joy. Now, across the full humanity that we want to be jubilant, fly your kisses.

It is a family fun in a family reverie shared with the other families. Children would like it between dinner and bedtime, say for India, 9.00 p.m. or any time as may agree. The evening prayer time is Hamilton's.

Our nuclear and terror brothers, their wives, and their kids too are welcome to join this love rally. All shall stand up and do a Heber yell. This is a symbolic goodwill initiative, an untried new get together, an unwalked virgin avenue, a modest dream march, marching toward a hope.

Roll the globe again. Bring the whole of mankind into your dream fold. A fresh love is releasing itself to all including the last baby born. Now in dream, you call out everyone, 'Hi! You, friend, turn to me, I love you. Let us hug one another and be a family, one family, all of us. Shall we be, dear?' Let everyone say this. Look at the globe and kiss the nations. One by one you do. And as you kiss, say, 'This world is ours, dear, ours given of God who loves us all. How blessed we are to live in that which is so beautiful.'

United against whatever is evil, we are emotionally knit. The scene that we behold is one of the universal deluge of love. The tattering aged ones, the middle-aged men and women, the dreamful boys and girls, the naughty smiling babes, the budding sweet cuties, and the angelic little ones. All meet our unseen friends all over the world in dream for fifteen minutes daily. In dream, we hug ourselves and kiss. Look into the faces intently, and whisper into the ears, 'We are one, dear. One.' Kiss them on the cheek, and kiss them again and again. And say, 'We are one, dear. One.' Kiss again. Look them into their eyes with as much love as you have. And smile a sweet smile. Then after one more smile, break up into our own individual selves and rise up into the dream space waving and wishing a sweeter meet tomorrow.

Till then, goodbye.

Printed in the United States
By Bookmasters